BULLETPROOF BRIDE

ALSO BY KIT MORGAN

The Prairie Bride Series

The Prairie Groom Series

Matchmakers in Time

Mail-Order Bride Ink

BULLET PROOF
Bride

BY

KIT MORGAN

the *Pink*
Pistol
SISTERHOOD

BOOK 4

Bullet Proof Bride

© 2023 Kit Morgan

Cover © Shanna Hatfield, https://shannahatfield.com

Edited by Ray Anselmo

License Note

1

The Weaver Farm train stop, Washington state, August 1900

G oldie Colson stared at the apple orchards as the train took on water. They'd been here a while. Her destination was Nowhere, a nothing town in Washington that was as far from her old life as she could get. On the one hand, that was a good thing. Her life in Kansas City was horrible. She'd lost her parents in a bank robbery less than a year ago and now her betrothed to a bunch of train robbers.

"Miss Colson?"

She looked at the elderly conductor with eyes red from crying. "Yes?"

"Are you sure you don't need anything? Something to eat? The folks that live here are bringing food for everyone."

Before she could speak, she noticed a giant of a man coming down the aisle. He was middle-aged with blue eyes and chestnut brown hair mixed with gray. He stopped when he reached them. "Howdy, ma'am. Name's Arlan Weaver. We heard what happened. Are ya all right?"

She couldn't help but laugh. "I just lost my intended and his father. No, I am not all right." She looked out the window again.

True, the men she lost she'd just met at a train station in Boise. She was a mail-order bride, and her betrothed Theodore Ferguson and his father Ben Ferguson, were off to visit Ben's sister in-law in Nowhere. The ride out of Boise was uneventful for a long time and she'd spent it trying to get to know her future husband. It was the same after they left Baker City, Oregon. She was liking the man she was about to marry when they entered Washington state. His father too, was nice and seemed caring. He found a pretty, mahogany box left on one of the benches at the train station in Baker City, and thought he saw its owner get on their train. Mr. Ferguson brought it along, peeked inside to see if there was any information about who it belonged to, and said it contained a firearm. He meant to speak to the conductor about it but dozed off. Then the train was robbed, and not all the outlaws escaped. "What is this place?"

"The Weaver farm, ma'am," Mr. Weaver said. "Maybe I oughta have my wife look at ya." He excused himself and hurried from the car.

Goldie watched him go, then went back to staring out the window. She didn't know how many passengers were in the other car. They were spread between two, her car carrying her little party of three and a few others. They had shot Theodore and his father while the rest of the passengers fled into the second car seeking refuge. She had no idea if anyone in the second car had been wounded or killed. She only knew what happened in this one. Three lay dead, one of them an outlaw.

Two more men entered the car, took one look at what lay in the rear seats, then headed that way. A woman followed. She was middle-aged, pretty, and had brown hair and kind brown eyes. "Hello," she greeted. "I'm Samijo Weaver. Why don't you come with me?"

Goldie nodded, too numb to do anything else. How had she survived? She should have been shot too. But fate intervened when her future father-in-law slumped in the seat in front of her, and she grabbed the gun out of his hand. The rest was a blur. She didn't remember firing the weapon, but obviously she had.

"Come along, now," Mrs. Weaver said gently. "Let's get you taken care of."

Goldie's lower lip trembled, and she bit it. She let the woman guide her from the seat and steer her off the train. With no home and no place to go anymore, Goldie didn't know what to do. But she was alive, and for now that was enough.

There was a bench on the tiny platform, and she sat as the conductor joined them. "If you'd like, you can ride in the second car with the others, Miss Colson. You were getting off in Nowhere. Do you have relatives there?"

She shook her head. "I don't. But the Fergusons did."

"Ferguson?" Mrs. Weaver said. "Were they coming to see Connie Ferguson?"

She nodded. "Yes. She's Ben Ferguson's sister-in-law."

"I see," Mrs. Weaver said. "She runs the hotel in Nowhere. She's remarried and known as Mrs. Hoskins now. Perhaps I should accompany you there."

Goldie stared at her a moment. "I... don't know."

Mrs. Weaver looked sympathetic. "Were they close, Mr. Ferguson and Connie?"

She shrugged. "To be honest, I don't know. He said he hadn't seen her in years. I was... his son's mail-order bride. We were to be married in Nowhere so she could attend the wedding and they could visit, then we were to move on to Seattle."

Mrs. Weaver sat beside her as another woman came onto the tiny platform, a basket in her hand. She stood off to one side and waited. She was beautiful with her dark hair and streaks of gray at the temples.

"Bella, bring the basket," Mrs. Weaver said. "Arlan?"

The big man came out of a tiny ticket office. "Yeah?"

"I think we should accompany Miss Colson to Nowhere."

"I'm sending a telegraph to Sheriff Riley now." He ducked back inside.

Mrs. Weaver smiled at her. "Are you hungry? Bella brought food. She's married to my husband's brother Calvin."

Goldie forced a smile and nodded. She wasn't hungry, but also knew she had to eat something. Who knew when she'd get another meal? She had no money of her own and had been at the complete mercy of her future husband and his father. They were going to Portland to work in a lumber mill. It was her one chance to start a new life and, dare she hope, find love? Now that chance was gone.

Mr. Weaver came out of the little train office. "I've sent word to the sheriff in Nowhere about what happened. He'll want to speak to ya, of course. And I agree with my wife, we'll accompany ya and help ya tell Connie." He glanced at his wife and back. "Um, do you have any money?"

Goldie shook her head.

"Well, considerin' yer betrothed ain't gonna need his, yer entitled to it. I'll see that ya get it and the rest of their belongings."

She looked at him. "Shouldn't Mrs. Ferguson get them?"

"Connie has herself a hotel to make money with," he said. "What have you got?"

She swallowed hard and looked at the platform. "Nothing."

"Well, there ya have it." He kissed his wife on the cheek. "Best get what ya need, darlin'." He headed for the train.

"I can't thank you enough," Goldie said softly.

Mrs. Weaver smiled gently. "You don't need to. Not after

what you've been through." She nodded at Bella. "The train will be ready to leave soon. Give her the food."

Goldie rose, a bit unsteady, and took the basket offered. She followed them to the second passenger car as a flicker of hope ignited in her heart. Perhaps there was still a future for her. But she wouldn't know until she got to Nowhere.

Once she was settled on the train, she placed the basket in her lap and clutched the handle. There was enough food in it to last a few days, and she noticed the other passengers had sandwiches and apples. No one said a word as they ate. Goldie looked at the basket and figured that since she lost folks, she got more food.

It wasn't long before Mr. Weaver came with several satchels that held her betrothed's and his father's clothing and effects, plus some money and a note from the conductor. It brought tears to her eyes when she unfolded the note and read it:

Miss Colson,
Use these twenty dollars as you see fit. Good luck.
Mr. Schwab

Taking a deep breath, Goldie looked at Mr. Weaver. "I don't know what to say."

He smiled. "Ya don't have to say nothin'. Just accept the kindness and use it to get a fresh start. I'm sure Connie will help ya too."

She bit her lip again, jaw trembling, and nodded.

He put the satchels and a pair of saddlebags in the basket overhead, then left the train. No one spoke to her, and that was fine. She didn't want to talk to anyone right now. Her every nerve was raw from the experience, and she wondered what would become of her now. Would her life stop or start in

Nowhere? She had no idea. She only knew she'd lost a chance at love. And she had a lot of love to give.

It wasn't long before Mr. Weaver returned with his wife in tow. "Like we said, Samijo and I will accompany ya to Nowhere. We know Connie and can introduce ya personally."

His wife sat in the seat in front of her. "We'll also speak to Sheriff Riley. After what you've been through, we decided you shouldn't have to go through this by yourself."

Goldie hiccupped and covered her mouth with a gloved hand. "I don't know what to say. You don't have to do this for me."

Mr. Weaver shrugged. "We've seen our share of trouble over the years, and let's face it, Miss Colson, yer all alone."

Goldie nodded. They had no idea. "Thank you." She pulled a handkerchief from her reticule and wiped her eyes. She couldn't believe their kindness.

Mrs. Weaver whispered something to her husband. He nodded and left the train again as she smiled at Goldie. "One of my daughters was nearby and ran to our place to fetch us each a change of clothes. Arlan's gone to get it from her."

Goldie managed a nod. She still couldn't believe the train had been robbed or that Theodore and Mr. Ferguson were gone. Maybe if she concentrated on that hard enough, she'd forget about how she'd shot one of the outlaws.

Mr. Weaver returned about ten minutes later with a carpetbag in his hand. He sat next to his wife and got settled.

She watched him with interest. He was a huge man, tall and broad through the shoulders. She never saw the farm but had heard about it from the conductor. He said it was enormous. "You raise apples," she said to no one in particular.

Mrs. Weaver shooed her husband out of their seat, then took the one across the aisle from her. "That's right. Along with pears, pine nuts, and a variety of other goods."

Mr. Weaver turned in the seat and smiled at her. "We also make milk powder, cheese, clothing and even hats."

Goldie tried to picture Mr. Weaver making a hat and couldn't manage it. "I… heard a little on the way here, just before…" She looked away.

"You don't have to talk to us if you don't want to," Mrs. Weaver said.

"That's all right, I think it might help." Goldie forced a smile, and the woman smiled back. "Do a lot of people live on the farm?"

"Yes, well over forty," Mrs. Weaver said. "Arlan is the oldest of four brothers."

He smiled. "There's me, then my twin brothers Benjamin and Calvin, and finally the youngest, Daniel."

"Forty people from four?" Goldie whistled before she could stop herself. "Oh, sorry, it's just that I can't imagine…"

Mrs. Weaver laughed. "Don't even try. We've had folks come and go, but you must remember, Arlan and I married a long time ago. Twenty-nine years, to be exact. Then his brothers got married and their mother got remarried, we had children and his brothers had children…"

Goldie smiled and nodded. "I'm sorry, I'm not thinking straight."

Samijo reached across the aisle and patted her shoulder. "You're going to be okay, Miss Colson."

She smiled again. "Thank you, Mrs. Weaver."

"Samijo."

"Goldie."

"We don't stand on ceremony 'round here," Mr. Weaver said. "Ya can call me Arlan if'n ya want."

"Thank you, but Mr. Weaver seems more appropriate." She smiled again at Samijo then settled more comfortably in her seat. It was a two-hour ride to Nowhere, and she would have to hold herself together. She didn't know if she'd have been able to do it more easily riding in a car alone, or in the company of the Weavers and the other passengers. Goldie only knew that she'd gone numb and had to stay awake. She feared that if she fell asleep, she'd see the shocked look on the outlaw's face the moment she shot him and relive the entire event all over again.

No, Goldie wanted to forget it had ever happened. Unfortunately, she knew that today had changed her life forever, and she'd never be the same.

T he train ride into Nowhere was uneventful. For this, Goldie was grateful. She could also see it in Samijo's eyes. The woman looked like she'd seen a lot, even if it was working a farm. She supposed a lot of things could go wrong: weather, accidents, the death of loved ones or live-stock, and many other things. She'd grown up in Kansas City herself and was unaccustomed to life's tragedies in rural areas. Yes, she knew death, her aunt and uncle and parents, but that was it. And for her, it was enough. It was why she'd become a mail-order bride.

Now here she was, in a little town in the middle of nowhere—called Nowhere, no less—with hardly a penny to her name. She could rummage through Theodore's belongings and his father's, but she didn't know how much she'd find there. Maybe some cash, and if she was lucky, train tickets to Portland, their final destination. But until she got settled and had some time to herself, she couldn't do much of anything. She was having a hard enough time processing what had happened.

"Here we are," Samijo said, a hand on Goldie's shoulder.

She gave it a squeeze, and Goldie had to admit it was comforting.

"Thank you for all you've done. Both of you." She smiled at Mr. Weaver, who had stood and was gathering things from the baskets overhead.

He handed Goldie her and Theodore's valises. "Shall I carry this one for you?" He held up her father-in-law's.

"If you don't mind. Thank you." Goldie scooted out of the seat then looked out the train windows. This station was bigger than the one at the Weaver farm and she hoped the town was too. Though the farm had a lot of people, it was still just a farm.

"Are you hungry?" Samijo asked. "I don't know if Connie has anything at the hotel. It doesn't have a dining room."

"But there's a mighty fine restaurant in town. Hank's. It's run by one of my nephews and his wife."

She forced a smile and nodded. "I don't know if I could eat. But thank you."

Samijo smiled sympathetically. "You should have something. It will make you feel better."

Goldie hugged her and Theodore's valises. "Let me get to the hotel first, then we'll see."

Arlan nodded toward the door at the end of the train car. "Samijo, take her to the hotel. I'll go speak to Spencer."

"Spencer?" Goldie asked.

"Sheriff Riley," Samijo said. "We've known him for years. He's a kind man and he'll help you as much as he can."

Goldie nodded again, then headed for the end of the car. As soon as they disembarked, she looked around the small train station. Other passengers were also exiting the train, and she realized she'd been alone with the Weavers. When had the others changed cars?

"The hotel is this way," Samijo said with a nod toward the platform stairs. They walked down a short street and into the main part of town. As Goldie looked around, she noticed how charming it was and smiled.

"Like what you see?" Samijo asked.

"Yes, I do. I come from a big city, so this is nice. But I'm not sure I could live in a small town."

"I've lived in both, and have to admit, I much prefer small-town living." Samijo smiled warmly and nodded down the street. "This way."

Goldie followed her as Mr. Weaver went across the street to the sheriff's office. She hoped this Sheriff Riley didn't ask her too many questions. She was having trouble remembering everything; it had all happened so fast. Maybe she shouldn't have done such a good job of trying to block the incident from her mind during the train ride. He would want facts, and she'd be obliged to give them.

But she wasn't the only one he'd be talking to. He'd want to ask the other passengers questions as well. Come to think of it, where were the other passengers? She stopped on the boardwalk and turned around. She didn't see anyone from the train behind them.

"Is something wrong?" Samijo asked.

"Where are the others?" She turned to Samijo with a worried look.

"They may be on their way to the sheriff's office." She pointed across and up the street. "See?"

Goldie looked, saw several other passengers she recognized, and noted they were indeed heading straight for the sheriff himself. He stood on the boardwalk speaking with Mr. Weaver. She watched as he pointed directly at her, then continued talking with the sheriff. "Thank you, I was worrying for nothing."

Samijo put an arm around her. "Spencer is very thorough. He'll question everyone, including you. Now let's go meet Connie." She steered her toward the hotel and they were off again.

The hotel, like the rest of Nowhere, was a charming structure, painted olive green with cranberry trim on the windows and spindle work. Inside it was just as quaint. The expression on the proprietress' face, not so much. She looked up from a book and glared at Samijo. "What are you doing here?" she asked with a hint of panic. "Land sakes, Samijo, don't tell me half the family has come to town."

"Not today, Connie." She stepped to the counter. "I'm afraid I have some bad news." She glanced at Goldie. "It's about your brother-in-law Ben."

She looked at Goldie, gasped, then turned back to Samijo. "Oh goodness, what happened?" She looked at Goldie again. "Who are you and where is my nephew, Theodore?"

Goldie shut her eyes against tears. "They're gone, Mrs. Ferguson. I'm so sorry, but they're gone."

Mrs. Ferguson backed up a step. "What do you mean, gone?"

Samijo went around the counter and took Mrs. Ferguson's hands in hers. "There was a train robbery, Connie. Your brother-in-law and nephew were shot."

The woman's hands flew to her mouth as she gasped again. "No." She turned away for a moment, pulled a handkerchief from her sleeve and wiped her eyes. "I haven't seen Ben in years. We were never close, but he was still some of the only family I had left. Land sakes, I only met my nephew a handful of times."

Samijo hugged her. "I'm so sorry for your loss. Is there anything I can do for you?"

"No, Samijo, but thank you." Mrs. Ferguson turned around and looked at Goldie. "You must be the mail-order bride Ben wrote me about."

Goldie's heart pinched with guilt, as if Theodore and his father's deaths were her fault. But they weren't, and she had to stop thinking they were. There was nothing she or anyone else could have done. "Yes, ma'am. I am. Goldie Colson."

Mrs. Ferguson looked her over. "Well, now what am I to do with you?"

"Connie," Samijo said firmly. "This poor thing has no one. She may have just met your nephew and brother, but with their deaths, well, I was hoping you could help her out."

Mrs. Ferguson's expression pinched again. "How? Don't tell me you want me to give her a job?"

"That's a brilliant idea, Connie. Why don't you?"

Mrs. Ferguson narrowed her eyes at Samijo. "I didn't say I was... I wasn't offering... oh, you Weavers!"

Samijo winked at Goldie. "Come now, Connie, you know you wouldn't mind some extra help for a while."

"I could work for room and board," Goldie suggested. "Until I can make enough money to move on. Won't you help me?"

Mrs. Ferguson sighed. "Very well, but I'll have to speak to Hoskins. He has some say in this."

"Does he work here?" Goldie asked.

Samijo smiled. "Hoskins is more than an employee, remember?"

"He's my husband," Mrs. Ferguson stated. "Now, I'd better show you a room. Far be it from me to turn you away." She arched an eyebrow at her. "After all, we were almost related."

Goldie's cheeks flushed. At least the woman hadn't tossed her out the door. She watched Mrs. Ferguson grab a key from a cubby behind her, then come around the counter.

"Follow me." She headed for the staircase.

Goldie heaved a sigh and followed, Samijo beside her. "Don't worry, Connie may come across as gruff but she's a real softie. She does like to gossip now and then, though."

Goldie smiled as they headed up the stairs. By the time they reached the landing, Mrs. Ferguson was several doors down on the right, inserting the key in a lock. "This can be your room for now." She opened the door and stepped inside.

Goldie stood before the entrance and peeked in. The room

was large with a bed, dresser, desk and chair, settee and table. "This is lovely."

"Go inside," Samijo urged.

Goldie entered the room and spied a door on one wall. "Closet?"

"Bathroom," Mrs. Ferguson said. "We have hot and cold running water now. I'm sure you'll enjoy it." She gave Samijo a pointed look.

"Don't worry Connie, Goldie will work hard and then some. Isn't that right, Goldie?" Another warm smile.

Goldie decided she liked Samijo Weaver. "I'll do whatever work needs done. Laundry, washing dishes..."

"We don't have a dining room," Mrs. Ferguson pointed out.

"Oh, yes, I forgot." Goldie went to the bed and set the valises down. "How many rooms does the hotel have?"

"Ten. We do a fair amount of business but could always be busier." She looked Goldie over again. "I suppose having an extra hand won't hurt for a while. Considering I don't have to pay you. Just feed you."

"Connie," Samijo warned. "A worker is worth their wages, are they not?"

Mrs. Ferguson rolled her eyes. "Okay, fine. Room and board and three dollars a week."

Samijo smiled in triumph. "That's more like it." She smiled again at Goldie. "How does that sound to you?"

She swallowed hard. "Very agreeable. Thank you, Mrs. Ferguson. From the bottom of my heart. And as soon as I have enough money, I promise I'll..."

"Leave, stay," Mrs. Ferguson said. "Makes no difference to me. Just see that you do a good job. This hotel has a reputation for being very respectable."

"That much is true," Samijo quipped. "And it has an interesting history." She winked.

Mrs. Ferguson gasped. "It does not."

Samijo raised her eyebrows at her. "Doesn't it?"

Mrs. Ferguson wrung her hands a few times. "Oh, all right, it does. But she's not going to hear any of that from me." She handed Goldie the key and marched out of the room.

Goldie stared after her. "What was that about?"

"It's a long story involving some of my family members, and of course Connie. You'll have to ask Hoskins about it. But right now, why don't we get you something to eat, then go speak to Spencer? Does that sound all right?"

Goldie nodded. She was suddenly exhausted and stared at the bed. It looked great right now. Still, she should eat something.

Samijo took her hand and led her to the door. "One of my nephews runs the restaurant, just as Arlan said. They have an interesting menu, as his wife Ichiko is Japanese."

Her stomach rumbled. "I can't wait to see what they offer, even if it is different."

"You'll find Nowhere is full of all sorts of surprises." She smiled again, and they left the room.

When they went out the hotel doors, Arlan was waiting on the boardwalk. "All settled in?"

"Yes, but not without the usual resistance from Connie," Samijo said.

"Is she always like that?" Goldie asked. After all, she would be working for her.

Samijo smiled. "It's like I said, she comes across as sharp, but she means well."

Goldie mustered a weak smile and hoped it was true.

3

R hys Miller entered Hank's Restaurant, spied Arlan
and Samijo Weaver at a table and stopped short. "Is
it Friday already?" Samijo usually came to town
every other Friday to make deposits and take care of other
farm business. Sometimes Arlan came with her. But this was
Wednesday.

Still, he headed for their table, locking gazes with the
pretty young blonde sitting with them. "Arlan, Samijo. What
brings you to town early?" He smiled at the woman. Now that
he was closer, he noted she was not only pretty but well-
dressed too. Was she visiting from back east? "You have
company?"

The lovely creature looked at him, her eyes rounded to
saucers. Had he said something wrong?

"Rhys, this here is Miss Colson," Arlan said. "She's had a
little trouble, and we accompanied her to town. In fact, Samijo
will bring her by the bank later…"

"Arlan," Samijo cut in. "I don't think Goldie's up to
speaking with Rhys today."

Arlan looked at Miss Colson. "Oh, yeah, I guess yer right.
One thing at a time." He gave Miss Colson a sympathetic

smile. "If'n ya don't mind, I'll speak to Rhys a moment." He left the table and nodded at the door.

Rhys took one last look at Miss Colson and Samijo, tipped his hat and followed. Outside he gave Arlan a concerned look. "What happened?"

"You'll hear 'bout it soon enough." Arlan sighed. "The train was robbed."

"What?!"

He nodded. "Yep, and Miss Colson in there lost her betrothed and her future father-in-law. Connie down at the hotel was their relation."

Rhys' jaw went slack. "I had no idea Connie had any relatives other than a niece. You never hear her speak of them."

"Well, she does, or did." Arlan's expression was somber. "Rhys, that little gal in there has been through a lot."

"I should say so. Poor thing. To lose her betrothed and…"

"She was a mail-order bride," Arlan said.

He stared at him a moment. "She was?"

"Yep, just met her intended a couple of days ago from the sound of it. Connie's offered to take her in for a time and let her work at the hotel. She'll need to set up an account at the bank so she can start savin' her wages. Then she can either stay on, or move on and try her luck in Seattle, which is where she and her betrothed were headin'. They were gonna stop here and get hitched so the father could visit with Connie and she could attend the wedding."

Rhys whistled long and low. "That poor woman."

"It gets worse."

His eyes widened. "How?"

"She shot a man."

His eyes popped wide. "What?"

Arlan held up his hand. "In self-defense. One of the outlaws." He glanced at the door. "I'm not even sure to call it that. She grabbed a gun out of her future father-in-law's hand and it fired."

"Hit an outlaw and down he went?"

Arlan nodded. "Somethin' like that."

Rhys rubbed the back of his neck. He could feel a headache coming on. "I'll help any way I can."

"That's mighty kind of ya. Maybe bring your ma by the hotel. Billie's been through something like this before."

Rhys nodded. His mother was British and came to America to make a better life for herself. Highwaymen had attacked her and her father and didn't come away unscathed. Grandpa Jones lost his life and Mother lost an eye. Half her face had been disfigured, but she was still a sight to behold and a prominent citizen of Nowhere. It didn't hurt that Father owned the bank. "I'll arrange everything. Miss Colson won't have to lift a finger. And I'll have Mother pay her a visit and perhaps invite her to dinner."

"She's gonna be mighty overwhelmed for a spell. Tell Billie not to rush her."

"Mother knows. She still talks about what happened the night she and my grandfather were set upon. I can't imagine what it's like to face such danger." He looked at the door to the restaurant again. His heart went out to Miss Colson. "What happened to the other train robbers?"

Arlan sighed. "They got away."

Rhys gaped at him. "No."

He nodded. "I spoke to Spencer a little while ago. He's pretty sure he knows what gang it is. This could get ugly, Rhys. I wouldn't be surprised if Spencer deputizes a few men to help him watch over the town for a spell."

He straightened. "I'll do it."

Arlan laughed. "You have a bank to run."

"During the day. But I'm free at night. I could patrol the town as well as anyone else in Nowhere."

"I have no doubt, but you'll have to speak to Spence. I suspect that if by some slim chance them varmints decide to pay Nowhere a visit, one of the first places they'll head is the bank. Wouldn't you rather be there to protect it?"

Rhys did his best not to look at the door again. The vision of loveliness on the other side needed help, and he'd give it. But Arlan had a point. His first duty was to the bank and his family. "Right. I will."

Arlan smiled. "Ya here for lunch?"

"I am."

"Then join us. Just don't expect Miss Colson to be too chatty after what she's been through."

He nodded and followed Arlan back inside. As soon as he was seated, he smiled at Samijo, then Miss Colson. "Arlan informed me you've had a rough day. I'll do whatever I can to make things easy for you, including opening an account so you can start saving your money. All you'll have to do is sign some papers and you'll be set."

Miss Colson blinked at him a few times, and he hoped her ordeal hadn't rendered her mute. Phoebe Manning, Arlan and Samijo's niece, had suffered some trauma when she was younger and lost her ability to speak for months.

"Miss Colson?"

"Yes," she finally said. "Thank you. You are most kind, Mister...?"

"Miller," he said with a smile. "Rhys Miller." He glanced at Arlan and back. "If you like, I think you'd benefit from speaking to my mother. She's been through a similar experience. I think she'd bring you comfort."

Her eyes misted, and she swallowed. "Thank you again." Her voice was barely above a whisper.

Hugh and Ichiko came to say hello, took their orders, then retreated to the kitchen. "Why is this placed called Hank's?" Miss Colson asked.

Rhys smiled. Maybe she was just trying to stir up the conversation. "After the previous owner. He opened this place decades ago and when he retired, he gave it to Hugh."

Miss Colson smiled. "How nice for them."

"Make no mistake," Arlan said. "My nephew can cook. Giving him this place was the best idea Hank ever had."

"I look forward to his cooking." As if on cue, her stomach growled.

Samijo smiled. "I think we're all hungry."

Miss Colson put her hand over her belly and blushed. "Oh, my."

"Don't be embarrassed," Rhys said. "I'm famished myself. I'm surprised my stomach isn't agreeing with yours."

She blushed again but said nothing. The poor thing. He wished there was more he could do to help, but for now, starting a bank account and letting her meet Mother would have to suffice.

When they food came, they ate in silence. Rhys stole glances at Miss Colson, and noted she appeared to be holding up, but after what she'd gone through, she was bound to break down at some point. He decided he'd get some things taken care of at work, then see Mother and let her know what happened. It was only a matter of time before it was all over town, and if Connie Ferguson had anything to do with it, it might be already. She could wag her tongue with the best of them. But as this involved her own kin, maybe she'd show some restraint and keep this to herself for a time.

The meal over, Rhys sipped his coffee as Arlan and Samijo told Miss Colson about the Weaver farm. Her eyes grew big at certain times, and she'd look at him for confirmation. He smiled and nodded the third time she did it and bit the inside of his cheek to keep from laughing. "Yes, the farm *is* that big. And you can believe everything they've said so far."

She openly gawked at them. "Goodness, I had no idea there was so much involved in harvesting apples."

"Ya stay in Nowhere long enough, yer more than welcome to come to the farm and help at the next harvest," Arlan replied. "Rhys has done it."

"I have." He gave Miss Colson the warmest smile he could muster. "It's a lot of work, but it's fun. We'd go on a Friday, spend a couple of nights, then come home Sunday afternoon after church."

"Church?"

"We have our own chapel," Samijo explained.

Miss Colson stared at her. "How many people live on your farm again?"

Arlan laughed. "Enough to have our own chapel, train station, and we're even thinkin' of building a schoolhouse. We got so many younguns runnin' around, it'd be a lot easier to teach 'em all in one place."

"Right now, we use the chapel," Samijo said. "But our pastor…"

Miss Colson gasped. "You have your own pastor?!"

"Yes, Rev. Wingate. He came to us as a travelin' orator and was more than happy to fill the position," Arlan said.

Rhys took in her wide-eyed look. "Don't worry, everyone wears the same expression you have when they hear about the Weavers. But they're good people, the lot of them, and you're lucky you met them when you did." He leaned a little closer. "You won't have to go through this alone."

She looked at him, blinked a few times and nodded. She looked about to cry, and he hoped she held herself together. He wasn't sure about Arlan, but he didn't know what to do with a crying woman. Land sakes, he couldn't handle it when Mother cried. Thank goodness she didn't do it often.

When they left Hank's, he accompanied Miss Colson to the door. "I'd be happy to walk you to the hotel."

She shook her head. "The sheriff will want to speak to me. I should go see him."

"It's on the way to the bank. I can take you there."

"We'll take her," Arlan said.

Samijo looked at Miss Colson, then Rhys. "Come now,

Arlan, it won't hurt to have Rhys along. Spencer might have some information about the outlaws Rhys will need."

Miss Colson sucked in a breath. "Why? Will they try to rob the bank?" She turned to Arlan. "You don't think they'll come here, do you?"

Rhys and Arlan exchanged the same anxious look. They were hoping the subject of the outlaws paying Nowhere a visit didn't come up. Arlan sighed as his hands went to his hips. "Let's talk to Spence. There's no sense getting' riled up for nothin'."

Except there was, Rhys thought. There were a lot of half-wit outlaws roaming the West and he hoped these were some of them. They usually steered clear of populated areas, preferring to rob individuals that lived far from town or a lone stagecoach. But these outlaws went after a train. That was something else, and they might have more than half a brain between them.

"Well, all right," Miss Colson said.

Rhys heard the shudder in her voice. She was scared, and he didn't blame her. She had to be shaken with all that had happened to her today. He couldn't imagine the shape she'd be in if she'd been married to her betrothed for years and had made a life for herself. To have a husband and father-in-law snatched away like that would be devastating. To shoot an outlaw, even on accident, didn't help. Would the remaining outlaws seek their cohort's killer? He had no idea. But Spencer might.

The four headed for the sheriff's office where they found Spencer speaking with his older brother Clayton. He'd been the sheriff before Spencer took over the position. The Rileys owned a decent-sized apple farm outside of town. It wasn't near the size of the Weaver farm but was too much for them to handle if both brothers stayed lawmen.

"Arlan, Samijo," Spencer greeted when they entered the office. "Rhys?"

He stepped forward and gave Miss Colson a reassuring smile. "We're here so Miss Colson can tell you what happened, and to find out who you think might be responsible."

Spencer looked at some wanted posters on his desk. "I have a good hunch." He looked at Rhys and Arlan. "And I hope I'm wrong."

4

Goldie's insides quivered. What did the sheriff mean, he hoped he was wrong? "Excuse me, but… who do you think robbed the train?"

He shoved two wanted posters across the desk. "Do you recognize either of these men?"

A chill went up her spine as she looked at the posters. "Oh… dear me."

"You recognize one of them?" Mr. Miller asked.

She glanced at the banker, unable to form words for a moment. All she could do was point. "H-h-him. That's the man I… that is… the gun…"

Arlan looked at the poster. "He got shot." He gave her a single nod.

It somehow made her feel better. At least he didn't blurt that she'd murdered the man. She didn't. The gun went off on accident, but it saved her life.

Sheriff Riley, hands on hips, stared at the wanted posters. "And the other one? Do you recognize him?"

She looked at the posters again. "It's hard to say, they were wearing masks."

"Then how do you know this fellow is the one that got shot?" Mr. Miller asked.

She glanced his way, and his blue eyes caught her own. He was a handsome man and a part of her wished she'd been his mail-order bride. "Mr. Weaver removed his mask after he, um…"

"I took it off the varmint before carrying him off the train," Arlan said.

"I see." Sheriff Riley pulled two more wanted posters from the small stack on his desk. "What about these two?"

Goldie studied them. "Maybe, yes." She gave the sheriff a helpless shrug. "To be honest, I'm not sure how many there were all together. I only know of the three that were in our car."

"Were there others?" Mr. Miller asked Arlan.

"According to the conductor and engineer, there were five, but these are the ones we're concerned with." He nodded at the sheriff. "Right?"

Sheriff Riley nodded back. "Yes."

"Why is that?" she asked. "Why not all of them?"

Sheriff Riley pushed the other two posters across the desk. This one, he's nobody, drifts from gang to gang. He'll be long gone. But these three." He pointed at the two previous posters, then the new one. "He's not only the ringleader of this gang, but the older brother of the man you shot."

Goldie listed to one side. Mr. Miller caught her. "Whoa, maybe you'd better sit?"

She fanned herself. "Yes, sit. Sitting is good."

He steered her to a nearby chair and helped her ease onto it. "Spencer, some water?"

"I have coffee."

"That'll do."

The sheriff went to the potbellied stove and poured her a cup. Mr. Miller took it and handed it to her. "Here, drink this.

It will calm your nerves." He turned to the sheriff. "Who are they?" He glanced at the posters then turned back to her.

She smiled at him, then looked at the sheriff. "Who did I shoot?"

Sheriff Riley drew in a breath. "Well, they're known as the Coolidge Gang. You shot Jonny Coolidge. His brothers are Herbert and Dale."

"You said there were three we need to worry about," Mr. Miller pointed out.

"The fourth is a cousin. Dilbert."

Goldie's face screwed up. "Those are horrible names for outlaws. They don't sound menacing at all."

"Trust me," the sheriff said. "They are. You experienced it firsthand." He came around the desk and stood before her. "I know you've been through a lot today, but if you don't mind a few questions, this won't take long."

She shook her head. "Ask me anything."

He pulled a small writing pad and pencil from his vest pocket. "Arlan tells me the train robbers boarded the train about an hour from the Weaver farm. Is that right?"

She nodded. "I'm sure the other passengers already told you."

"Yes, but I still need to question everyone." He scribbled something on the pad. "Now, as best as you can, tell me what happened."

She took a deep breath and noticed Mr. Miller had maneuvered behind her. Knowing he was there made her feel safe. She was in a sheriff's office with three tall, capable-looking men. She didn't know if Mr. Miller was, in actuality, all that handy with a gun or his fists, but he comforted her all the same. Goldie told the sheriff the same thing she'd told the conductor and Mr. Weaver. What few passengers were in the car with her had already spoken to the sheriff and their stories matched.

"It was an accident, pure and simple," the sheriff said. "Still, I know how horrifying it must have been for you."

She nodded. She wanted nothing more than to soak in a hot tub and crawl into a bed. Fear made for a poor bedfellow, and she hoped she could relax enough not to go to bed tonight terrified.

"Spencer," Mr. Miller said. "Will they want revenge?"

The sheriff watched her a moment. "Even if you think their names are anything but outlaw worthy, it doesn't mean they won't try. These men have all done some mighty bad things. Even murder."

Her hand flew to her chest. "I see." Her heart pounding, she closed her eyes and concentrated on just getting through the rest of the day.

"But one never knows," the sheriff continued. "The Coolidges might hightail it to Oregon or over the border into Canada."

"Or come here," she said as she opened her eyes.

He shrugged. "It's hard to say, but if it makes you feel any better, I'll hire on some volunteers to help keep an eye out."

She took a deep breath and let it out slowly. "That does. Thank you."

Mr. Miller raised his hand. "I'd like to volunteer."

Sheriff Riley smiled. "You already did, remember?"

Goldie turned in her chair to look at him. "You did?"

He gave her a sheepish smile. "Well, it's the least I can do. We enjoy our little town, Miss Colson, and no gang of outlaws is going to come riding through here and spoil all that we've built up. We like to think of Nowhere as a peaceful place to settle. Who knows, you may grow to love it as much as the rest of us and stay."

She forced a smile. She had no idea what she was going to do. The prospect of marriage had brought her here, but now that was gone. She fought the urge to wring her hands. "Did you need anything else, sheriff?"

"No, that's it for now."

"Good," Arlan turned to Samijo. "We'd best let Aunt Betsy know we're here."

"You have relatives in town?" Goldie asked without thinking. Normally she wouldn't pry, but if she kept talking, her mind wouldn't have the chance to latch onto all the sheriff had said. She didn't want to think about a band of outlaws with terrible names riding into town to shoot her.

"Yes," Samijo said. "Our relatives own the mercantile in town. Would you like to see it?"

"Perhaps later. I'd like to return to the hotel if you don't mind."

"Not at all," she said.

"I can take you," Mr. Miller offered. He stood to one side now, wearing a concerned smile.

"Thank you, that's very kind." Goldie stood, set the coffee cup on the desk, then gave Sheriff Riley a parting nod. "Wh-where did the other gentleman go?"

"My brother?" the sheriff said. "Clayton went to round up some volunteers." He glanced at Mr. Miller. "I'll have him add Rhys to the list." He shook Arlan's hand, then Mr. Miller's, before he addressed her again. "Don't worry none, Miss Colson. You're in excellent hands."

She took a shuddering breath and hoped it was true.

They left the sheriff's office and parted ways. The Weavers headed down the boardwalk while she and Mr. Miller crossed the street. "Where is the mercantile?" she asked.

"Just a few doors down from the hotel."

She glanced across the street and wondered why the Weavers were walking on that side. Did they not want to get dragged into a conversation with Mrs. Ferguson at the hotel? Hmmm. "Mr. Miller, what can you tell me about Connie Ferguson?"

He stopped them in the middle of the boardwalk. "Oh,

yes." He cleared his throat. "Connie… well, she's not as bad as she used to be."

Her eyes widened. "Bad?"

He made a face. "Gossiping. But don't worry, Nellie Davis still holds the honor of being the worst gossip in Nowhere."

She fought against a sigh. "That makes me feel so much better."

His eyebrows knit. "It does?"

She shook her head. She might as well be honest with him. "So, my betrothed's aunt likes to spread gossip."

"But not as much," he reiterated as they continued their way.

When they reached the hotel, she stopped at the door. "Thank you for escorting me. I'm fine from here."

He looked at her and almost smiled. "I'll have my mother call on you tomorrow. Connie won't mind." His eyes flicked to the hotel doors and back. "And don't let Connie badger you into doing things you don't want to. She'll see how far she can push a person."

She shook her head at him. "How do you know all this?"

He smiled. "I was born and raised here. I've known Connie all my life."

She smiled. "That's nice to know. Thank you."

"My pleasure." He tipped his hat and left.

Goldie went inside, saw no sign of Mrs. Ferguson, and hurried up the stairs. Once she was in her room, she decided to take a bath as planned and try to relax. She didn't know what she was going to do and maybe she could think of something while she soaked. Thank goodness the Weavers had got her this far, and the townspeople were friendly and willing to help.

As the tub filled, she emptied Theodore's valise. There were a couple of changes of clothes, some money and their marriage contract. It was safe to say her future husband had little.

She did the same with Mr. Ferguson's belongings. He too carried only a couple changes of clothes, a little money, and of course, the mahogany wooden case he'd picked up in Baker City. She noticed it had brass hinges and a lock. "Hmm, I wonder if there's a key."

She set it on the bed and stared at it a moment. All she knew was that there was a gun inside. Good. She could use one about now.

She tried the box and gasped when it opened. The interior was made of green velvet and contained a pink-handled pistol. She took the pistol from the box and studied it. She knew a bit about firearms and could see that it was a .32 caliber Smith & Wesson with nickel plating and of course, had a pink mother-of-pearl handle. The passenger that left it behind in Baker City must be a woman.

"Well, aren't you a pretty thing? How much are you worth?" She spied something else in the box and picked it up. It was a piece of parchment. "What in the world...?" She read what looked like different snippets of handwriting. "*A gift from the great Annie Oakley, this pistol carries a legacy of love. If you possess this pistol and find love, please record your name and a bit of your story to encourage those who follow.*"

Goldie blinked a few times. "What?" She glanced at the box, then the pistol, then continued to read. "*Tessa James married Jackson Spivey on March 3rd, 1894 in Caldwell, Texas.*" She studied the pistol again. "Texas?" She returned to the piece of parchment. "*I was aiming for his heart but accidentally winged him in the arm. Thankfully, forgiveness and love cover a multitude of mishaps.*"

Goldie couldn't help it, she laughed and read some more. "*Rena Burke wed Josh Gatlin on June 2, 1894, in Holiday, Oregon – When my trousers and target practice didn't send him running, I knew true love had hit the perfect target for me.*"

Her laughter continued, and she hoped no one could hear her. She probably sounded like a madwoman.

"Kristalee Donovan wed Captain Johnny Houston on August 31, 1899, in Hugo, Indian Territory. With a little help from the pink pistol, both of us learned what love really is and will treasure that love forever. How new and bright life has suddenly become. Can there be any adventure more wonderful than this?"

Goldie stared at the pistol in her hand and let the parchment drop into the box. As strange as the pistol and notes were, this could be a blessing in disguise. Her chance at love was gone and she very much doubted a pistol could help her find some. But with said pistol in her possession, she might make it through this in one piece. Now all she had to do was hope that Herbert, Dale, and Dilbert didn't find her. Though if they did, she'd be ready.

5

Rhys poked at his dinner that night. "What's wrong?" his mother asked.

He looked at her and smiled. She was the only woman he knew who wore an eye patch. The scars on her face were clear above and below it, but no one in Nowhere cared if Billie Miller was scarred, blind in one eye, and wore the patch. She was a wondrous, beautiful person and everyone in town loved her.

"Rhys?"

He sighed. "Just thinking."

"About what?" Father cut his pot roast and popped some in his mouth.

"You're worrying for nothing," Mother said. "Still, I'll talk to the young lady. I remember what it was like to lose my father to a band of bloodthirsty outlaws. And to think this poor young woman lost two..." She cocked her head. "Oh, wait, she'd only just met them. Am I right?"

Rhys nodded. "Yes. I don't know all the details, but she was to marry Connie's nephew."

"Have you spoken to Connie?" Father asked as he scooped up some mashed potatoes.

"No. Though I do plan on going by the hotel tomorrow to bring her some flowers and offer my condolences."

"Flowers are always nice." Mother got back to eating, looking contemplative. She was a thinker and would be trying to figure out what to say to Miss Colson when she saw her.

"You could go with me," he said. "I'm sure Connie would like that."

"Connie Ferguson likes it when she gets any sort of attention," Father said. "I'm sure she'll have her fair share with this. I just hope she doesn't take advantage of it."

"Come now, Lucien," Mother said. "She's not that bad."

"She can be," Rhys and his father said at once. They laughed and got back to eating.

"So, is this Miss Colson pretty?" Mother asked, eyes fixed on her plate.

"Mother…," Rhys huffed.

"Well, you can't blame me for asking. After all, just last week you brought up the idea of finding yourself a nice girl to marry, and now one's practically been dropped in your lap." She shook her fork at him. "Why not get to know her?"

"Mother, she just lost her betrothed and her future father-in-law."

"Whom she didn't really know," Mother cut in.

Rhys sighed. He didn't dare get Mother going about marriage. She'd follow him around talking about this young lady or that one. Unfortunately, they were too young, or too old. There wasn't a lot of in between in Nowhere. None that he was interested in, that is.

The meal over, he went outside to the front porch and sat. His family lived in a lovely home on the edge of town, and he thought about building his own house. He didn't want to crowd his parents, especially when he and his bride (whomever she may be) had children.

He looked down the street toward town. He could build it at the other end of Nowhere. There were a few lots for sale, including one just outside of town with a small apple orchard. It would be fun to walk to his parents' house with his children and wife for Sunday dinner every week.

He smiled at the thought as Miss Colson popped into his head. She was pretty with her blonde hair and big brown eyes. Petite too. What a horrible thing to see your future husband and father-in-law shot in front of you. He wished he could do more for her, but he wasn't sure what.

He paced the porch a few times. Mother was right, she might be a delightful prospect, but he doubted she'd stay in Nowhere. If she was heading to Seattle, she'd most likely continue her journey as soon as she was able. Too bad. She was mighty pretty.

He leaned against the porch railing and looked at the darkening sky. He didn't like the idea of the Coolidge brothers coming here looking for her. It was a good possibility, and he wanted to be ready in case he was needed. Problem was, he wasn't very handy with a gun. There was never a need to be around here. Nowhere was just that, because it was nowhere close to a big city.

The people here were simple farmers, ranchers, with a few businessmen in town to provide what people needed. The town had one church, a doctor, a school, a mercantile, a post office, a bank, and a train station. It was also surrounded by apple orchards, good farmland, and had the mountains to the north and west. Tucked amidst orchards, farmland and forest, it was a hidden jewel that no one paid attention to, and folks here liked it that way.

He looked toward town and wondered if Miss Colson would come to like it too or head off as soon as she was able.

"Here you are," Mother said as she stepped onto the porch. "What are you doing out here?"

"Just thinking." He faced her and smiled. "Is Father engrossed in his new book?"

"Of course. I thought you'd be reading too, but here you

are. What's bothering you?" She sat on the porch swing and gave it a shove to get it moving.

Rhys watched her a moment then sat beside her. "Do you wish you had more children?"

She looked at him and smiled. "I will, one day. When you marry." She winked.

"But do you wish you had them now?"

"Oh, son." She patted his leg. "You will find a young woman one day, marry and have children of your own. Then I will be exceedingly happy. Both for you and for me. But especially for me."

He laughed. "I'll do my best. But don't get your hopes up with the woman that's in town. I doubt she'll stay."

She nodded wisely. "I know. But a mother can always hope."

He smiled, kissed her on the cheek, then left the swing. "I think I'll join Father and read."

She sighed, smiled back, then stood. "Me too."

He offered her his arm and together they went into the house. Tomorrow he'd introduce his mother to Miss Colson and hopefully she could help the young woman through any trauma she might have suffered because of her ordeal.

THE NEXT DAY, Rhys helped his mother pick flowers from the garden, put them in a vase, then walked her to the hotel. Inside, Connie was at the front counter going over a ledger with her husband, Hoskins. "Good morning, Rhys, Mrs. Miller," he called. "What brings you to the hotel?" He glanced at the staircase. "Is it our guest?"

"That's part of why we're here," Rhys said.

Mother stepped forward. "I brought you these, Connie dear. I'm sorry to hear about what happened. I dare say, I didn't know you had a brother-in-law."

Hoskins shook his head and sighed. "They were estranged."

"Still," Connie said forlornly, "it's a shock." She sniffed at the flowers then began to rearrange the blooms. "My poor nerves are shot, you know. They may never recover."

Rhys and his mother exchanged a quick look. Connie was already putting on a show.

"Your nerves are fine." Hoskins nodded at the staircase. "Are you here to see her?"

"If you're referring to Miss Colson,' Mother said, "then yes."

"Go on up, but don't drag her off somewhere for hours," Connie said. "I'm putting her right to work."

"Work?" Mother said, confused.

"Yes, that no-good brother... oh, um, Ben had nothing, and neither did Teddy, my nephew. I doubt Miss Colson has much either, which is why I did the charitable thing and took her in. She'll work in the hotel until she's earned enough to move on."

"That's very generous of you," Rhys said. He thought Miss Colson mentioned something about work yesterday, but he'd been thinking about what happened and how she appeared so... composed, that was the word, considering what had happened. But maybe she was still in a state of shock. Doc LeCarr told him what could happen to people who were in shock. Sometimes it wasn't pretty.

"Shall I fetch the young lady for you?" Hoskins asked.

Rhys smiled. "If you'd be so kind."

"Certainly." He crossed the lobby and hurried up the stairs.

Rhys went to a nearby chair and sat. Connie began speaking to his mother as he eyed the staircase. If the outlaws tracked poor Miss Colson here, would they burst through the doors of the hotel, grab her and be off? Would they even go through the trouble of abducting her or exact their revenge on the spot?

He shifted in his seat as his heart pounded. He was getting himself riled up and had better stop thinking about it. But he couldn't help himself. For whatever reason, Miss Colson brought out every protective bone in his body and he didn't even know her! It had to be more than her pretty face. There was something different about her, something… vulnerable. Should he try to find out what?

Hoskins came down the stairs with Miss Colson right behind him. "Here you are," he said when he reached the last step.

Rhys left his chair and went to the counter. "Miss Colson, it's so nice to see you again."

She gave him a shy smile, then noticed his mother.

He motioned to her. "Miss Colson, may I present my mother, Billie Miller."

Her eyes widened. "Billie, what an unusual name. I like it."

Mother smiled and offered her a hand. "Thank you. My name is really Jane, but my father called me Billie all the time."

Miss Colson shook her hand. "It's nice to meet you."

"Perhaps we could take a walk? I believe we have a few things in common."

Miss Colson looked at each of them as if expecting someone to say something to the contrary. Instead, they watched her, including Rhys.

"I know it's strange," Mother said. "You just met me. But I've been through something like what you have and thought perhaps I could help."

Miss Colson breathed a sigh of relief. "I see. Yes. Though I'm not sure what you can do for me. What's done is done, I can't undo any of it."

"No, you can't, but you can share your burden. I'd like to help you with it if I'm able."

Miss Colson's lower lip trembled slightly, and Rhys' gut twisted. Those outlaws had better not come to Nowhere. He fought the urge to make a fist—if he did, he'd want to hit something. "Why don't you take Miss Colson for a stroll to the mercantile, Mother?"

"A good idea. Have you been?"

"No, not yet." She smiled shyly.

Rhys relaxed a notch. "I'll escort you both," he offered. He wasn't about to let her go outside by herself. What if one of those lowdown snakes was lurking about?

"Well, if you're going to Quinn's," Hoskins said, "I'll head that way too. We need a few things. Connie, you'll be all right?"

"Of course, I will." She glanced at her flowers. "But hurry back. And bring me some candy for my nerves."

Hoskins narrowed his eyes playfully then smiled. "Of course, my dear." He opened the hotel doors wide for the rest of them and motioned everyone onto the boardwalk.

Rhys stepped out and waited until Hoskins closed the doors behind them. "Mrs. Quinn will probably ask a lot of questions."

"Oh, yes," Mother said. "Poor Betsy is inquisitive. She's also old and a little hard of hearing. Her son and daughter-in-law run the mercantile but Betsy's often in the storefront."

"I'm sure she's heard what happened," Miss Colson said. "I know people came into the hotel and spoke with Mrs. Ferguson."

"They did indeed," Hoskins said. "Old habits die hard when it comes to Connie, and everyone in town knows the story by now, but only you can tell us if what we've heard is true." He smiled warmly. "After all, you were there."

Rhys watched Miss Colson for any sign of distress. She looked a little apprehensive, but that was it. Good. Because it was all he could do not to loop her arm around his and keep her close at his side. Good grief, he'd just met the woman! What was he going to be like after she'd been in town a few days?

6

Goldie entered the mercantile, unsure what to expect. She was used to the dry goods stores in Kansas City and had a feeling that the little store in Nowhere would fall woefully short of what she was used to.

"Well, now," an old woman said from behind the counter. "If it isn't my wonderful niece and nephew come to call."

Arlan snorted as he and Samijo entered the storefront from a side hall. "We got those chores done ya wanted us to do." He smiled at Goldie. "Mornin'."

"Good morning." Goldie studied the old woman as she came out from behind the counter and kissed Arlan and Samijo on the cheeks. She was tall, thin, and had her white hair pulled back in a chignon. She had to be in her eighties, maybe even older.

"Come here, young lady," the old woman said. "Let me have a look at you."

Goldie glanced at Mr. Miller, who gave her an encouraging smile." Go ahead," he said then smiled at the old woman. "Mrs. Quinn, may I introduce Miss Goldie Colson."

"Oh, no need to be so formal, Rhys," she said with a dismissive wave. Her eyes softened as she studied Goldie.

"Arlan and Samijo told me what happened to you, young lady." She shook her head. "What a shame." She took Goldie's hands and patted one. "You should know that the folks around here are mighty supportive of their own. We'll help you out as much as we can. I can give you some store credit if you need it."

Goldie shivered from the chill going up her spine. She wasn't one to attract attention to herself and had been getting more than her fair share the last day or two—first meeting Theodore and his father, and now all this. "Thank you, but I have a little money."

"Do you need anything from here?" Mrs. Quinn asked.

She looked around. The store might be smaller than what she was used to, but it had a little of everything. "If I do, I'll know where to come." She tacked on a smile and hoped the woman left things at that. She needed a few items but had to be careful with her money.

"Since we're here, why don't you pick up some necessities?" Samijo suggested. "Don't worry about the cost, we'll take care of it."

"Oh no," Goldie whispered, "I couldn't let you do that." She looked around the store again, noticed the man behind the counter and forced another smile. "Besides, I'm not sure what I need."

"There are certain things everyone needs," Mr. Miller said. "Betsy, would you do the honors? She was a mail-order bride." He winked.

Mrs. Quinn—Betsy—gasped in delight. "Don't mind if I do."

"Oh, dear me." Samijo shook her head with a smile.

"What is it?" Goldie noted Betsy had gone behind the counter and was digging through a stack of boxes.

Samijo smiled mischievously. "Aunt Betsy and her friend Leona Riley love to equip mail-order brides. Leona is Sheriff Riley's mother. They did it to me when I first came to

Nowhere, and let me tell you, I still cringe when I think about it."

Goldie's eyes widened. "Why?"

"I left here with so many things I couldn't believe it." Samijo looked her in the eyes. "Their generosity overwhelmed me. Half the goods I left with, they didn't charge for. A wedding present, they said. The rest Arlan took care of."

Arlan nodded. "It's true. If Leona was here, they'd be goin' plumb loco with happiness at havin' a bride to outfit."

"But I'm not a bride," Goldie said. The pink-handled pistol popped into her head, and she pushed the thought aside. Like *that* was going to do anything for her situation. Except protect her, that is.

"Even if you're no longer a bride," Mr. Miller said. "You'll need some things to help you settle in. Wouldn't it be nice not to have to worry about spending what money you have on things like tooth powder?" He maneuvered in front of her. "Trust me, let us do this."

She wrinkled her nose, a nervous habit, and took in their expectant faces. All three looked eager to spend their money. That only made her feel more uncomfortable. "No, really, none of this is necessary."

"Nonsense." Samijo went to a far wall, grabbed a chair, and brought it to one end of the counter. "If you'd like, take a seat. Otherwise look around, see if there's anything you think you might need."

Goldie wiped away the tear forming in one corner of her eye and forced another smile. Her family wasn't well to do by any means, but they'd had decent shelter, food on the table, and some savings. She took that savings and found something to rent while she looked for a job. Unfortunately, she couldn't find reputable work that would keep a decent roof over her head. Rather than move into some shack passing for a house, she did the only sensible thing she could think of. She became a mail-order bride.

Now here she was, in Nowhere, Washington, stranded, almost penniless, and working for someone that would have become her relative if her future husband hadn't been shot dead by train robbers. She had a few changes of clothes, a little money scraped together from the deceased, and a pink-handled pistol with a lot of strange claims of being able to bring love to the owner. The thought still made her laugh.

"Go ahead," Mr. Miller urged gently. "Gather what you need."

"Or watch Betsy do it for ya," Arlan added.

She gaped at him then looked at the growing pile of goods on the counter. "What in the world?"

"We told you," the others said at once.

Mr. Miller laughed. "They did the same thing to my mother when she came to town."

She looked at him in shock. "They?"

"Betsy and Leona."

"Oh, yes, there's two of them." Goldie stared at the pile, then went to the chair Samijo brought for her and sat. She still couldn't think straight, and if the old woman wanted to put together a few things for her, she wasn't going to argue. "I'll pay you back."

"No, you won't." Arlan looked at Mr. Miller. "And neither will you."

"But Arlan," Mr. Miller said, closing the distance between them. "She's going to need more than this."

They both looked at the goods on the counter. There was a hairbrush, comb, and a hand mirror. Betsy was adding bars of soap, shampoo, and hairpins. There was also a can of tooth powder, a small bottle of perfume and a couple of hand-kerchiefs.

Tears stung Goldie's eyes as she realized it would take her a while to pay the Weavers back, even if they said she didn't have to.

"You're fretting," Mr. Miller stated beside her. When did he join her?

"Am I?" she squeaked. She cleared her throat. "You are too kind."

"We're just being neighborly." He bent to get eye level with her. "You've been through something many of us can never comprehend. It's the least we can do while you're here." He straightened. "And who knows, maybe you'll take a liking to our little town and stay."

She scoffed. "And do what, Mr. Miller? Be a scullery maid in the hotel?"

"There are other things here you could do. Mrs. Davis is about to retire from the post office. Perhaps you could take her position."

"The post office? And will that keep me housed?"

His eyes met hers, and she couldn't read him. Well, other than the pity she saw etched in his features. Goldie didn't want that from him. She wanted a solution to her problem. Yes, she had a job for now, but how long would it last? Mrs. Ferguson might decide she didn't need a person working for her after all and boot her out.

"Stop worrying. Everything will be fine."

She looked around the store and noticed his mother standing off to one side speaking quietly with Hoskins. She'd been quiet since they arrived, and Goldie wondered why. Maybe she was waiting to speak with her alone and biding her time until then.

By the time Betsy was finished, the pile on the counter had grown substantially. The old woman had even added a bolt of light yellow calico. "Do you sew?" She measured out the fabric.

"Yes, of course." She left the chair. "Really, is all this necessary?"

Betsy waved a pair of scissors at her. "Just because you ain't getting hitched like planned, doesn't mean you can't enjoy a few things."

"Arlan," Mr. Miller said. "I'd like to help."

He sighed. "Oh, all right. We'll split it."

Goldie fought another chill. She hated them making all this fuss.

Mr. Miller and Arlan went to the counter and paid for the goods as Mrs. Miller approached. Was she going to add anything? Goldie hoped not.

"Matthew, would you mind delivering this to the hotel?" Hoskins asked.

The man behind the counter smiled and nodded. "Of course." He began to wrap items in brown paper. Goldie studied him a moment. He must be Betsy's son. He was middle-aged, with brown hair streaked with gray, and wore spectacles.

"I'll put everything in your room," Hoskins stated. "Oh, and Matthew. I need a few items when you're done wrapping Miss Colson's things."

"Sure, do you have a list?" Matthew smiled at her then took a list from Hoskins. Goldie wondered why everyone, including Connie, called him by his last name.

Mr. Miller said something to his mother, then smiled at her. "There, you're all set. I must return to the bank, but my mother will take good care of you."

"And we have a train to catch," Arlan announced. He smiled at her too.

Goldie fought against tears. "You're leaving?" She didn't know why she was getting upset. She hardly knew these people. Yet they came to her rescue and stayed by her side until now. Of course she didn't want them to go. It meant she'd have to face whatever came next alone.

"We have to, but we'll return next week." Samijo smiled at Mr. Miller. "I'll have banking to do. In the meantime, we know we're leaving you in expert hands."

"You'd better get your things together if you're going to

catch the morning train home," Betsy called from behind the counter.

"C'mon, Samijo," Arlan said. "Let's do as Aunt Betsy says."

Samijo said something to Mrs. Miller before joining Goldie at the counter to give her a hug. "You'll be all right, you'll see."

She shuddered, unable to help it, and hugged her back. "Thank you, for everything. I'll repay every cent."

Samijo smiled. "No, dear, you won't. But you could help us with the harvest if you have time."

"When is that?"

"Soon enough." Arlan gave everyone a parting nod, then escorted Samijo down a hall and disappeared.

"Where are they going?" Goldie asked.

"They stay here whenever they're in town," Betsy said. "It's the only time I ever get to see them. I don't venture out to the farm much unless I get a hankering to see my sister Mary. You'll meet the entire clan if you help with the harvest."

Goldie could only stare. She'd never heard of such a thing. The Weaver farm was a good two-hour train ride from Nowhere, yet folks went all that way to help at harvest time? No one around Kansas City would do such a thing. At least, not that she knew of.

"Are you all right, dear?" Mrs. Miller asked.

Goldie nodded. Everything was so surreal; she didn't know what to think at this point.

"Good, then let's take a walk." Mrs. Miller looped her arm through Goldie's.

"Where are we going?"

"To my house to have tea. It will be quiet there with the men gone and we can have a pleasant chat."

Goldie glanced at the counter and her pile of goods. Matthew was just wrapping the two handkerchiefs and the hand mirror in brown paper. Maybe she ought to take the handkerchiefs now. She had a feeling she was going to need them.

7

They left the mercantile and headed back the way they came, passing the hotel, the sheriff's office and the street that led to the train station. Goldie noticed the post office, a tiny little structure that couldn't be more than seven feet by ten. She didn't relish the thought of spending all day in such an enclosed space and wondered if this Mrs. Davis read a lot. How much work could there be in a town of this size? She'd never be able to support herself as the postmistress.

"You were a mail-order bride?" she blurted without thinking. She didn't want to think any more than she had to at this point. Mentally she was exhausted.

"Yes, but only because I couldn't find a husband in England. So, my father and I came here."

Goldie tried to study Mrs. Miller out of the corner of one eye. She was tall, almost six feet, and buxom, all curves and muscle and height. Most Englishmen probably didn't find her appealing, especially with the scars on her face and the eye patch. But she spoke proper English, held her head high as she walked, and possessed a bearing that only came from confidence in one's self, privilege or both. "How did you become a mail-order bride?"

Mrs. Miller smiled. "The same as you, I would imagine. I found a matchmaker. In my case, Mrs. Adelia Pettigrew. An eccentric woman, to be sure, but she could match two souls perfectly. I still write her on occasion and let her know how things are going."

Goldie was silent as they passed the bank. Like the rest of the town, it looked quaint, untouched by the sort of men that robbed trains. "Do you like it here? Is it different from England?"

"Oh, very. But it wouldn't matter where I lived so long as I was with my Lucien. He was looking for someone of my stature and intelligence. And with Mrs. Pettigrew's help, found me."

They were close to the edge of town, and Goldie saw a few houses up ahead on the right. The road split there. "Where does that lead?" She pointed to the left.

"The Riley farm, and a few others. We're going this way." She headed right toward the homes. My house is the third and last house until you reach the Davises'. Mr. Davis used to own the bank until Lucien, his manager at the time, bought him out."

Goldie followed along, studying the lovely homes as they went. The third was a little bigger and just as charming. "How long have you been here?"

"Oh, my, let me see. Since spring of 1877. When I came here, I feared Lucien would take one look at me and send me back. I had scars from my ordeal, and not just the ones on my face."

They reached the porch, and Mrs. Miller led her inside. "Have a seat in the dining room, dear, while I make some tea." She led her through a parlor into a dining room and waved at the table before continuing through another door to what Goldie guessed was the kitchen. She studied the room and sighed. This was the sort of home she'd always wanted. Not too big, not too small, cozy and comforting. The Millers' house was all of that and then some. If the walls could talk, they would surely tell her that this was a safe place to be.

It wasn't long before Mrs. Miller returned with a tray laden with a teapot, cups, and saucers. She set everything out then excused herself once again. When she returned this time, it was with a plate of cookies.

Goldie sighed. How long had it been since she'd enjoyed such a simple thing as tea with someone? She'd lost most everything in the fire that killed her parents, sending her into a tailspin of trying to survive. Thankfully, some of her clothes had been at the launderers, as were some of her mother's. She sold a few dresses and kept the rest, then did what she could to get extra money before her parents' savings ran out. Now she would have to make a life for herself and had very little to do it with. How would she survive?

"You look troubled," Mrs. Miller commented as she poured.

Goldie blinked back tears. She was no coward, but it was getting harder and harder not to let herself have a good cry. But to do that, she wanted to be alone. She thought the tears would come last night but didn't. She slept fitfully but managed to get a few hours rest.

"Are you?" Mrs. Miller prompted.

Goldie sniffed and fought the urge to wipe her eyes. "Who wouldn't be in my position?"

"Where were you heading after you married?"

"Seattle."

"Do you still wish to go there?"

Goldie clasped her hands in her lap and stared at the table. "I'm not sure. It's what Theodore and his father Ben wanted."

"Seattle is a big place to be when you're all alone." Mrs. Miller handed Goldie a cup and saucer. "Consider staying in Nowhere."

She closed her eyes. "That's easier said than done. Mrs. Ferguson didn't seem optimistic taking me on. I have no idea how long how long she'll let me stay and work at the hotel. What if after a few weeks she tells me to get out?"

"You're her nephew's betrothed."

"I was," Goldie pointed out."

"True, but Connie's not heartless. She's standoffish, but she'll warm up to you soon enough. Connie had her niece Ottilie working in the hotel when I first came to town. She worked for Connie for a number of years and was so happy. I think you'll remind her of Ottilie and bring back some of that joy."

Goldie sipped at her tea. It was hot and tasted wonderful. "What happened to her niece?"

"She married and wound up moving away." Mrs. Miller stirred sugar into her cup. "Who knows, maybe you'll settle here, find a nice young gentleman, and get married."

Goldie almost sprayed tea all over the table. She coughed and sputtered a few times before she patted her chest with her hand. "Went down the wrong way."

Mrs. Miller smiled. "Of course. Do be careful."

Goldie fanned herself with a hand. Whenever anyone mentioned love or marriage, she'd think of that blasted pistol. Well, there was nothing to it. Maybe Ben Ferguson was going to give it to Theodore as a wedding gift if he couldn't find the owner. Considering the pink handle, it was more likely he was going to give it to her. Maybe it was a family heirloom. But… what about the dates on the parchment? Not to mention the locations.

"Are you quite recovered, dear?" Mrs. Miller asked.

"Yes, thank you." She cleared her throat then had another go at her tea. Mrs. Miller was eyeing her over the rim of her cup, and she did her best not to fidget. She wished people would stop looking at her like she was a china doll about to break.

"I mentioned my scars earlier," Mrs. Miller said. "I hope you don't mind me saying this, but you'll have some." She sighed. "For me, I hit one of my assailants with a rock as he slashed my face."

"I shot one of the train robbers." Goldie stared into her teacup. "I don't feel anything."

"Neither did I."

Goldie looked at Mrs. Miller. "But you only hit him with a rock."

"Yes, that much is true." Mrs. Miller reached for a cookie. "And then his friends showed up and carted him off, leaving me hiding behind a log, wounded and bleeding. Trust me, that can leave scars."

Okay, she had Goldie there. "Yes." She continued to stare into her cup. "Mrs. Miller?"

"Mm, dear?"

"Did they heal?"

"My scars? Yes. It took some time, and if not for Lucien, I might still have them. I was frightened, nervous all the time, and plagued by nightmares. He rescued me from all of it."

Goldie raised her head and met the woman's gaze. "How?"

Mrs. Miller smiled. "He loved me."

Goldie's gaze returned to her cup. No one was going to love her to healing from what happened. She'd have to do this on her own. The question was, how? By relying on the towns-people of Nowhere? She didn't know anyone in town and was barely an acquaintance of the Weavers. She had no friends here, no family.

She wiped away a tear. Drat! She didn't want to start crying now. Not while she was with someone.

Mrs. Miller set down her cup, came around the table and took the chair right next to Goldie. "Go ahead, dear. Let it out."

Goldie shook her head, trying to hold back the flood ready to spring forth. "I… can't."

"I understand, but what do you hope to gain by not giving in to your grief?"

"I didn't know Theodore yet, or his father. I'd only been with them a few days and we talked so little…" She sniffed back a tear and shut her eyes.

A hand was suddenly over hers. "My dear child, you lost not only your future husband, but a dream. You've suffered not two deaths but three."

Goldie opened her eyes and stared at her. She was right. Her grief wasn't just about the Fergusons, but what they represented. A life of her own with a husband, a home, children. And in a flash, it was all gone. A sob escaped, then another. "Oh, Mrs. Miller, wh… what am I going to do?"

She smiled, pulled Goldie into her arms, and held her. "First, you're going to have yourself a good cry, then you're going to help me make some lunch for my husband and son."

Goldie sucked in a breath, trying to regain control, but it was no use. The tears came, and she wasn't sure when they'd stop. She sobbed against Mrs. Miller's shoulder, glad for the woman's comforting words. Mrs. Miller didn't care that they were strangers, she was there for her in the best way she knew how and let Goldie have her first good cry since yesterday's ordeal.

When she was spent, she took the handkerchief Mrs. Miller offered, wiped her eyes, and gave her a tiny nod. "Thank you."

"You're welcome, my dear. Feel better?"

She nodded then blew her nose. "I'm sorry about that…"

"Don't be. You needed it. You can't hold things like that inside. If you do, it will cause you all sorts of mischief. I know it did me."

She sniffed back more tears and nodded. "You didn't want to talk about what happened to you with Mr. Miller?"

"I didn't think I had anything to cry about. Time had passed since the incident on the road that killed my father."

Goldie's eyes popped wide. "What?"

Mrs. Miller nodded. "Yes, dear. They killed him. And my father's dying wish was that I find a husband, marry, and live a good life."

Goldie froze. "And you did."

"Yes." Mrs. Miller scooted her chair back and stood. "Now, mind helping me in the kitchen?"

"But what about Mrs. Ferguson?"

"Connie? Don't worry about her. If I have to, I'll help you do whatever work she had planned today."

Goldie's shoulders slumped in relief. "Thank you."

Mrs. Miller smiled and motioned toward the kitchen door. "Come along, let's make Lucien and Rhys some sandwiches. They'll be home for lunch soon."

Goldie nodded and got to her feet.

"Fetch me a loaf of bread from the bread box," Mrs. Miller said as they entered the room.

Goldie studied the bright, cheery kitchen. Would she ever have a place like this along with a husband and family? She scanned her surroundings, found the bread box, and took out a loaf. "Would you like me to slice it?"

"Please do." Mrs. Miller went to an icebox and began to rifle through the contents. When she was done, she brought a plate of sliced ham to the table and a few small jars. They made the sandwiches in silence and Goldie hoped she wasn't taking up too much of the woman's time.

Before she could lament further, she heard men's voices in the dining room. Mr. Miller entered the kitchen, a happy smile on his face, followed by a handsome middle-aged man.

"Lucien, Rhys," Mrs. Miller said. "You're just in time." She went to the kitchen table and set the plate of sandwiches down. "Lucien, this is Miss Goldie Colson. She'll be having lunch with us today."

"Well, how nice," her husband said. "Rhys has told me all about you, Miss Colson. I hope you'll find our little town to your liking."

Rhys (she would have to think of him by his first name to keep them straight) pulled out a chair for her. "Please, sit down."

"Thank you." She did and scooted in the chair. As soon as everyone was seated, Mr. Miller said the blessing, then the meal began.

Goldie had a sense of calm she didn't before and smiled at Mrs. Miller every time the woman looked her way. She was right. Having a good cry instead of holding it back made her feel better. Maybe trying to handle this alone wasn't the brightest idea after all. But be there a shoulder to cry on or not, she still had a long way to go if she was to survive this.

8

It was all Rhys could do not to stare at Goldie… that is, Miss Colson. She sat across the table from him, a vision of loveliness. She looked like she'd been crying and probably had. Mother had a way of comforting those that needed it most and knew how to deal with someone who had been through the unspeakable. As much as he'd love to ask his mother about her time with Goldie, he knew it wasn't his place. The conversation would have been private, and Mother wouldn't tell him a thing if that was the case.

He finished his sandwich and watched Goldie (why not just call her that?) nibble at hers. He hoped she had some sort of appetite—it would mean she wasn't as bothered by the things that had happened. If she stopped eating, that might be a problem, but nothing he or the rest of his family couldn't handle.

"Rhys has seen to an account for you, Miss Colson," Father said. "I hope you don't mind that he took the liberty."

"Not at all." She met his gaze across the table. "Thank you."

Father cleared his throat. "You'll want a savings account as well, correct?"

"Yes." Her eyes were still locked with Rhys', and he did his best not to look away. It gave him a chance to study her while his mother and father got back to eating. Her eyes were a bright blue, her hair like spun gold. Her name was fitting, and he wondered if her mother and father were also blondes.

"Rhys?" Mother said. "Did you hear me?"

"Huh?" He blinked, breaking eye contact, and turned to his mother. "What was that?"

"I asked if you were going to the Weavers' to help with the harvest next week."

"Oh, yes, I... planned on it." His eyes had locked with Goldie's again and he gulped.

She smiled shyly and looked away.

"You'll have to be sure everything's caught up at the bank before we head out." Father smiled at Goldie. "Talk to Connie and find out if she and Hoskins plan on going."

"Will they leave the hotel unattended?" Goldie asked with concern. "What if they want me to take care of it? I know nothing about running a hotel."

"I wouldn't worry, dear," Mother said. "If they venture out to the farm, then they'll leave the hotel in good hands. Right, Rhys?"

He sighed. "You mean my hands. Or Charlotte's." He smiled at Goldie. "Seems I'm the only one they trust to run the place when they're gone. If not me, then Charlotte Quinn from the mercantile."

"Oh, I see. Well, then. I won't worry." She sighed in relief and nibbled at her sandwich again.

Rhys smiled in response. She was scared, poor thing, afraid of being alone and left with nothing. Well, he'd see about that. He didn't know why he was drawn to her. Maybe it was because she was so vulnerable right now and needed protection. He'd see she got that too. In fact, he'd better speak to Spencer again about either being deputized or start taking a shift to patrol town. If the outlaws that robbed the train did indeed come here, then it wasn't only Goldie that was in danger—everyone was. They'd have to stop them and quick before anyone got hurt.

Finished with the meal, he drank the iced tea Mother offered, then left the table. "I'd best get back to work. Miss Colson, would you like to come with me? I'll need your signature on a few things."

"I should get back to the hotel. Mrs. Ferguson must be getting antsy about now wondering where I am."

"She's not antsy until she comes banging on our door," Father said with a laugh.

"That's very true." Mother stood and began to clear the table. "Run along, dear. Take care of your business at the bank. If Connie gives you any grief, tell her to come speak to me."

She didn't look convinced. Rhys cleared his throat to get her attention. "Trust me, just the mention of my mother will do the trick."

"Well, okay, then." She left the table. "Thank you, Mrs. Miller. You've been very kind."

Mother smiled. "Now when you have the chance, you can bring comfort to someone else that needs it. Pain often recognizes itself in others. They may not look like they're hurting on the outside, but you'll see it."

Goldie slowly nodded. "Thank you again."

She followed Rhys through the house to the front door. "I hope my mother wasn't too hard on you."

"Hard on me? Not at all. She's a very gracious woman. And so kind."

"Yes, but she can still strike terror into the meanest person. I don't know how she does it." He did, though. She was almost as tall as he was, for one, and well-versed in the fine art of verbal warfare. He should warn Goldie never to get into a debate with her.

They headed for the bank and Rhys tried not to look at her. He did steal a few glances and bit his tongue to keep from asking things he shouldn't. She was probably tired of people inquiring about the incident on the train and could do with a rest. "I'll accompany you to the hotel when we're done at the bank. If Connie's smart, she won't work you at all today and let you recover."

She nodded and said nothing.

"Unless of course you want to keep busy." He raised his eyebrows at her. "Do you?"

"In all honesty, I'm not sure what I want, Mr. Miller."

He smiled. "I know it might not be proper where you come from, but around here, we're all on a first-name basis."

She stopped, stared at him a moment, then continued. "How strange. Rhys."

He smiled. "Yes, well, Nowhere isn't your typical town. Though we're not as, um, different, that's a good word... we're not as different as Clear Creek in Oregon. That town has a reputation for strange things."

"I've never heard of it."

He shrugged. "It's just as well." He was looking for things to talk about but gave up when they reached the bank. It was time to keep to business. They entered, went into his office, and he motioned to a chair. "Have a seat."

She studied the space. "I've never been in such a small bank."

"Nowhere is a small town," he countered with a smile. He wasn't going to mention that this used to be a storeroom. Father had the only real office in the building, but when he appointed Rhys bank manager, he thought he could do with an office of his own.

He shuffled some papers around and found hers. "You'll sign here and here." He pointed to the signature lines on the account application.

She stared at them a moment. "I've never had a bank account before."

His eyebrows shot up. "Never?" His eyes flicked to the papers. "May I ask how old you are?"

"Twenty."

He smiled and handed her a pen. "Well, here's to your first."

To his delight, she smiled back, took the pen and signed where he'd indicated. "There," she said. "All done."

Rhys put the papers back into the stack, then came around the desk. "Now, off to the hotel." He led her through the bank and outside. No one said a word as they started down the boardwalk. He didn't expect them to. The bank had only three employees, Father, himself, and Charlie Winthrop the teller. People had already heard about what happened and knew he'd set up an account for Goldie. But after a few days, folks would figure she'd settled in, and would start talking to her. She might even get a few dinner invitations.

When they reached the hotel, he stopped them at the door. "Maybe I should handle this. After all, you've been with my family all morning and its well past lunchtime."

"I can handle myself," she said and faced the door. Before he could say another word, she marched inside.

Connie stood behind the counter wearing a sour expression. Rhys had seen it a thousand times before. It was just the way Connie looked. Her mouth always curved down, no one knew why. Her eyes were a bit too close together, and her eyebrows, like her mouth, were spaced in a way that she looked like she was frowning all the time.

Goldie approached the counter. "Mrs. Ferguson. I'm back. I spent a lovely morning with Mrs. Miller and was invited to lunch with them. Now I'm yours. What did you have for me?"

Connie didn't say a word. Instead, she fixed her eyes on him. "What are you doing here?"

"I escorted Miss Colson home," he said matter-of-factly.

"Oh, well, okay." She looked Goldie over. "You can sweep and mop the kitchen floor for starters."

"Starters?" Rhys said. "Connie, yesterday was very trying for Miss Colson." He smiled at Goldie—maybe he should use her first name in front of Connie. "Goldie should rest."

"Goldie, is it?" She narrowed her eyes. "Hmmm." She came out from behind the counter. "Maybe a little work will do her good. Sweep and mop the kitchen floor for me, then you can have the rest of the day to yourself. But tomorrow, I'll show you how things are done around here."

"Very well, Mrs. Ferguson." Goldie gave him a nod. "Thank you for escorting me back."

"It was my pleasure. Are you sure you'll be all right?"

"Yes."

He tipped his hat. "Afternoon, then." His gaze lingered, and it was all he could do to make one foot move and then the other. He stopped at the door and smiled at her. "Good day." He tipped his hat again and left.

Outside he exhaled, then marched across the street to the sheriff's office. Spencer was inside sitting behind his desk, writing out a report. "Rhys, what are you doing here?"

He sat on the other side of the desk. "How do I get deputized?"

Spencer's eyebrows rose as he leaned back in his chair. "I can swear you in, but are you sure you want to do that?"

"I am."

Spencer shrugged. "Well, okay." He opened the top drawer of his desk, pulled out a deputy's star and slid it across the desk. "Raise your right hand."

Rhys did. "Now what?"

"Repeat after me. 'I, Rhys Miller, do solemnly swear to protect the town of Nowhere from those that would do it and its citizens harm.'"

Rhys repeated everything, then scratched his head. "That doesn't sound very official."

Spencer shrugged. "It does to me." He took a pencil and tapped Rhys on the shoulder. "You're now an official deputy."

He laughed. "What was that?"

"Well, it's not exactly a knighthood, but it'll do." He smiled. "You got a gun?"

He cringed. "No. There was never a need for one."

"Well, around here, when you're the law, they come in handy." He went to a cabinet against the wall and opened it. "I've got a spare pistol here." He looked over his shoulder at him. "Don't suppose you have any bullets?"

Rhys shook his head. "No gun. No bullets."

The sheriff nodded good-naturedly. "Fine, I'll load it and give you some bullets, but you should go to Quinn's Mercantile and get yourself a gun belt."

Rhys nodded. "I have shot, just so you know."

"Yes, I know, which is why I'm surprised you don't own a gun."

He shrugged and left things at that. He could get a little target practice in over the next few days. "Have you informed Deputy McKay of the train robbers?"

"I have. He's scouting around today to see if they've camped anywhere in the area."

"Would you like me to help him?"

"No, I think it's best you stay in town and look after your bank."

Rhys noticed he said nothing about Goldie, but that was okay. He'd rather stay in town and make sure things were okay here than be away if something happened. "Fine." He took the gun from Spencer and looked it over.

"I'd spend some time with that, get a feel for it." Spencer handed him some bullets, then returned to his desk. "And Rhys? You don't have to wear the badge. Just carry it with you."

"But if I'm an official deputy, shouldn't I wear it?"

"I'd rather not give anyone reason to panic. Wear it only if you need to."

Rhys nodded in understanding, then headed for the door. Spencer was still worried, which meant there was still a good chance of the train robbers showing up in Nowhere. Maybe he ought to get in some target practice now.

9

oldie swept and mopped the floor, then did some dusting in the Fergusons' private parlor. She was about to retire to her room when Hoskins suddenly appeared in front of her with a feather duster of his own. "Miss Colson."

She started, then nodded. "Forgive me, but you gave me a fright."

"I do apologize. I'm very light on my feet." He motioned her to sit. "Please."

She took the chair indicated and smiled. "Thank you, Hoskins, for letting me…"

He wagged a finger at her. "*Mr.* Hoskins."

She blinked. "What? But I thought…"

"Everyone calls me Hoskins, even Connie." He dusted the mantle. "I was a head butler at one time in a very large household. Then I came here and… well, let's just say the rest is history." He turned to her. "But here we are. And I hope you stay on."

"But I've hardly started working."

"You're working now."

She smiled. "I'm, er, sitting."

He looked at her with raised eyebrows. "So you are." He chuckled, then went back to dusting the mantle. "I suppose you're wondering why Connie is still referred to as Mrs. Ferguson?"

"It did cross my mind." She smiled. He was such an odd fellow.

"Well, Nowhere is a small town and no one really got in the habit of calling her Mrs. Hoskins." He winked. "And yes, some call me Mr. Ferguson."

Goldie giggled. "So long as you don't mind…"

"Oh, I don't. No one here is confused by it. I suppose an outsider like yourself might be." He gave her a sly look.

What was he doing? No matter, she was enjoying the conversation. "How long have you been here?"

"Me? Oh, a little over four years." He stopped dusting, a far-off look in his eye. "Has it really been that long?" He smiled, more to himself than to her. "Well, now that we're getting to know each other, you might as well look at your list of duties. I've taken the liberty of writing everything down for you. Certain things are done on certain days to keep things shipshape around here." He smiled sadly. "I'm afraid Mrs. Ferguson and I are slowing down a little. We could get by without the extra help, but it takes us a lot longer to get things done."

She caught the sadness in his eyes and wondered if one of them was in worse shape than they were letting on. "I'll do whatever I can. Just let me know what that is."

His smile returned. "Splendid. I'll fetch the list. I left it in the kitchen."

He disappeared and Goldie slumped in her chair. She'd been in Nowhere a little over twenty-four hours and concluded that it was the strangest town she'd ever been in. It was wonderful that the residents were so friendly, but to have Rhys and the Weavers buy her so many things that morning… then there was Mrs. Miller. Was she an angel? Goldie smiled at the thought. Mrs. Ferguson was crabby looking, but from the sounds of things, she wasn't a mean person by nature.

When Hoskins returned, he handed her the list. "Sundays you'll have free, but there are duties to be done the other six days of the week."

She looked at the list and her eyes went wide. "Mr. Hoskins, is ironing your clothes the usual duty of hotel staff?" She arched an eyebrow at him.

"Oh, um, well, if you have time. We don't launder our guests' clothes or iron them. But Connie…" He wiggled his fingers. "Arthritis, you know."

"I see." She returned her attention to the list. "Clean the rugs in your private quarters?"

He shrugged. "It *is* part of the hotel."

She sighed and got back to reading. "Cook? But you don't have a dining room."

He shrugged again. "Yes, but we must keep up our strength for the sake of our guests." He batted his eyelashes.

Goldie stared at him slack-jawed. "I suppose these are all the chores the two of you perform on a day-to-day basis not only for the hotel, but yourselves?"

He flinched.

"Mm-hm." She closed her eyes in resignation. They didn't want an employee, they wanted a slave. Would she even get paid?

"You can start tomorrow bright and early by making everyone breakfast," he announced happily.

She looked at him and sighed. "Mrs. Ferguson told me I would help with the hotel, nothing more. I will not be taken advantage of."

He held up both hands as if she had him at gunpoint. She almost wished she did. "Now, now, Miss Colson. Can I help it if my wife added a few things to the list?"

She rolled her eyes. "Sir, I will help with the hotel for room and board, but I won't be your maid, cook, laundress…"

"What's going on in here?" Mrs. Ferguson stomped into the parlor. She saw the list and marched to Goldie's chair. "What's that?"

Goldie smiled at Hoskins and handed her the list.

Mrs. Ferguson started to read. "Hoskins!"

He looked appropriately sheepish. "Now dear, I was just trying to make your life easier."

She spun on him. "She is not your personal servant, nor mine."

"I… well… oh, blast."

Goldie bit her lip to keep from laughing. Either Hoskins had grown lazy in his old age, or he really was trying to watch out for his wife. Currently, he was well chastised and red as a beet. "So I won't be making breakfast."

"Heavens, no,' Mrs. Ferguson snapped. "I don't even know if you can cook."

Hoskins began to slink toward the door.

"And you!" She grabbed his arm and dragged him back to the center of the parlor. "Apologize."

"But dearest…" he whined.

Goldie's eyes were watering with the effort it took not to laugh. Nowhere was the oddest little town she'd ever encountered or probably ever would. "I've swept and mopped the floor as you asked and did some dusting. Will that be all?"

"Yes, Miss Colson. Take the rest of the afternoon and rest." Mrs. Ferguson gave her a heartfelt look, the first she'd seen from the woman. "Take a walk, explore the town, nap, whatever you wish." She frowned at her husband. "And as for you, we're going to have a little talk about slipping into old habits."

To Goldie's surprise, Hoskins gulped. Land sakes, what was that about?

Mrs. Ferguson steered him toward the kitchen. They disappeared through a door to leave her gaping after them. "My goodness." Goldie left the parlor, went up to her room, and tried to lie down. That lasted all of ten minutes. She was restless and decided to explore the town.

She left the hotel and started down the boardwalk toward the mercantile. When she reached it, she debated whether to go inside, then decided against it. One visit that day was enough. She walked to the edge of town and kept going. The road wound around an apple orchard and there was something almost magical about it. Where did the road lead, what would she find if she followed it? Mrs. Miller didn't say if there were farms out this way, but she imagined there must be. Who else owned the orchards on this side of town?

She walked for about ten minutes, realized she was quite alone, and turned around, a chill going up her spine. She didn't have the pink-handled pistol with her and didn't feel comfortable being by herself without it. At least she could shoot. She wasn't sure about anyone else in Nowhere. She hadn't noticed any of the men wearing gun belts except Sheriff Riley.

When she reached town she walked to the other end, noting the side street that led to the train station. There was a dressmaker's shop and a few other businesses on it but other than that, Nowhere was mighty small. She went down another little side street where a few houses were located and sighed. "Well, so much for my tour."

Goldie turned around and looked across the street at the bank. Rhys Miller's handsome face flashed before her. He had to be one of the nicest men she'd ever met. She stood and thought of the Weavers and their farm. She'd like to visit it one day but wasn't sure when she'd have the time considering the size of Hoskins' list... oh, wait. She smiled. That list wasn't the correct one.

"Mercy me. Could I live in a place like this?" She sighed as she slowly made her way to the main street. The town was charming, but full of quirky residents. They all had stories, she supposed. She certainly did. Maybe she should consider staying. For all she knew, the town was full of people whose stories were very similar to hers.

She found herself in front of the sheriff's office and sat on the bench outside. The town's main street was quiet with hardly a soul out tending to business. Maybe they were all home preparing the evening meal already. She wondered if the town had a library. She wouldn't mind reading something this evening but didn't want to spend her money on a new book.

Had Theodore been a reader? She'd never got the chance to ask him. She didn't get to ask him a lot of things. She was too shy at first, and they had just been warming up to each other when the train was robbed.

Mrs. Miller was right. The robbers took more from her than her future husband. They took her dreams. Would she ever get them back?

She was about to return to the hotel when she spied Rhys coming out of the bank. Her heart skipped at the sight of him, and she wondered why. She supposed it was because he was so easy to talk to. Should she speak to him now?

He saw her, waved, and headed her way. "Well, looks like I will." She smoothed her skirt and waited. Maybe she didn't want to be alone, and that's why she was restless.

He approached with a cheerful smile. "Goldie, it's nice to see you." He looked around when he reached her. "Out for a walk?"

"Finishing it." She looked up and down the street. "There's really nowhere to walk to."

"Yes, that's Nowhere for you." He smiled and tried not to laugh.

She smiled too. "Yes, I know."

He shrugged playfully. "May I escort you back to the hotel?"

"No, thank you. Does the town have a library?"

"Yes, a small one. Come with me." He led her back to the

main street and up the only other side street in town, the one that led to the train station. "Here we are."

Goldie looked at it. The town library wasn't much bigger than the post office and was next door to the dressmaker's shop. "It's open?" There was no sign to indicate it was a library.

"Sure." He went to the door and opened it wide. "Help yourself."

"But… where's the librarian?"

"Don't have one."

"Wh-what? You mean people take a book, read it, return it and that's it?"

He smiled. "Well, last I heard, that's how a library works."

"But surely you need a librarian?"

"No. Everyone's on the honor system and it works fine here."

She tried not to gape at him and failed. "Where do you get the books?"

"Donations, mostly. Sometimes we get lucky, and someone leaves a book behind on the train. That's always exciting as its usually something none of us have read."

She gulped. "Really?" She pressed her lips together. She would not laugh. "Well, I'll go inside and see what I can find, shall I?"

He nodded and waved her through the door.

She smiled at him, entered, and decided that as soon as she could, she was heading for Seattle and civilization. This place was too bizarre for her.

10

Several days later, Rhys thought he saw a stranger pass by the bank. He rushed out of his office, cut across the bank front and out the door. When he reached the boardwalk, there was no one there. "Well I'll be," he muttered. He stomped back into his office. Should he close the door? Charlie the teller probably thought he'd gone around the bend. But he knew better than to ask questions and would leave him alone.

He got back to work, his mind going over the last time he saw Goldie. She was sweeping the boardwalk in front of the hotel wearing a white apron. She was a vision of loveliness, and it was all he could do not to ask if she wanted to join him for lunch. Unfortunately, Connie came out and ushered her inside before he got the chance. He wondered how Goldie was getting along with Connie and Hoskins and figured that since he hadn't heard anything, things must be fine.

There came a knock at the door. "Come in."

Father poked his head in. "What were you doing a moment ago?" He stepped inside and closed the door.

Rhys rolled his eyes. "I thought I saw a stranger. I was wrong."

Father shook his head in dismay. "You're more nervous than a cat in a room full of rocking chairs. You've got to stop." He crossed his arms. "Are you sleeping?"

"My sleep is fine. *I'm* fine." Rhys stood and came around the desk. "It's just that I'm a little worried."

"About Miss Colson?"

"It's not just her. What if the men that robbed the train come to town and try to rob the bank? Or what if they harass some farmers and ranchers outside of town?"

"Well, I pity the poor fool that tries to harass the Riley farm. Especially if Clayton and Spencer are home. And I don't want to even think of what will happen if they're fool enough to try anything at the Weavers'." Father sat in the chair in front of Rhys' desk. "Besides, the farmers and ranchers I know all have guns."

Rhys leaned against the desk. "You don't. And you own the bank." He knew Father couldn't argue with that.

His father shrugged. "No, but I'd get one if I thought I needed it."

Rhys looked at the floor. "Spencer gave me one when he deputized me." He met his father's inquisitive gaze. "I can use it, but it's not to my liking. Care to do some shooting with me?"

"When I have time, son. Right now, I've got work to do and so do you." Father eyed the stack of papers on Rhys's desk. "Best get to it." He left the office for his own.

Rhys sat, stared at the paperwork, and sighed. He knew he needed to get it done, but he also wanted to get some practice in. The problem was he couldn't find anyone to give him pointers. Spencer was an excellent shot, so was his brother Clayton. As to the rest of the townsfolk, the only other person good with a gun was Deputy McKay.

He left his desk, checked with Charlie to see how business was, then excused himself for lunch and headed out. When he got to Hank's Restaurant, he stopped at the door.

Miss Colson was coming down the boardwalk straight for him.

"Mr. Miller," she said when she saw him. "What are you doing here?"

"Getting a bite to eat. You?"

She held up a piece of paper, and he noted she was still wearing her white apron. She must have left in a hurry. "I'm getting some lunch for Connie and Hoskins."

He smiled. "And how are the three of you getting along?"

A giggle escaped her. "Well enough. Though we have almost come to blows a few times. Connie is not saying much. And neither is Hoskins, but I take it he has some sort of past?"

Rhys laughed. "Goodness, you have no idea. Do you have a little time?"

"I think so. Connie sent me here to order sandwiches and take them back to the hotel."

He smiled, then opened the door for her and they went inside. "Let's get a table and we'll order. While we're waiting, I can tell you a little story." They perused the menus, gave Ichiko their orders, then Rhys smiled at her. "All of this is common knowledge, so I'm not gossiping."

She laughed. "All right. Let's hear it."

"Well, about four years ago, there was a little incident at the Weaver farm."

"The Weavers?"

He nodded. "Yes. Thatcher, who is the son of Calvin and Bella Weaver… Calvin is Arlan's younger brother if you'll recall?"

She nodded. "Go on."

"So, Thatcher was doing something out in the woods, hunting rabbits, maybe, and came across a young woman. She had a head injury, and Thatcher had to carry her all the way back to his family's house."

Goldie gasped. "Oh, dear me. What happened? Where did she come from?"

He smiled. She was enthralled so far. "Well, they patched her up and when she came to, she couldn't remember who she was. She didn't know her name, where she came from, anything."

Her hand flew to her chest. "That's terrible."

"Indeed. As time went on, she managed to get some of her memory back but very little. In fact, they didn't know what to call her, so they nicknamed her Mia."

"Well, that's not too bad," she said. "Was anyone looking for her? Did she have family?"

He smiled. "Oh, yes. But the ones that showed up to retrieve her weren't her *real* family."

Her eyebrows shot up again, but she said nothing.

"Hoskins, along with a woman by the name of Klump and two other gentlemen, came to the Weaver farm." He leaned toward her across the table. "They were her abductors."

She sucked in a breath and sat back. For a moment he thought she might fall out of her chair. "What?!"

"Now it's not as bad as it sounds. They were bumbling abductors at best, and in the end, all repented of their ways and have been productive citizens ever since."

Goldie stared at him; her mouth half open. "I'm working in a hotel with a man that abducted someone."

He whiffled his head. "No, you're working in a hotel with somebody who has redeemed himself in the eyes of the town, including Sheriff Riley and Judge Whipple."

"There's a judge in town?"

"No, we're not big enough for one. But we have judges that come through once a month."

She pinched the bridge of her nose. "Goodness gracious, I can't believe you told me all this."

Rhys shrugged. "It's common knowledge, Goldie. Everyone in town knows the story."

She lowered her hand and stared at him. "What about Mia? Did she ever get her memory back?"

"Yes, and her actual family showed up to claim her. A rich and prominent couple from Seattle. But Mia didn't want to go with them. Instead, she married Thatcher, lives on the Weaver farm, and comes to town now and then with some of her other relatives." He sat back with a smile. "You ought to go with us to the farm to help with the harvest."

"When is this harvest?"

"It started this week and is often quite the adventure."

She stared at him as if she didn't believe a word he said, then sighed. "I doubt Connie will let me go."

"Why not? If you get your work done in time, she should."

"That's just it, I work every day but Sunday. How could I accompany your family with my schedule?"

"Get some help, get your work done in half the time, and then go."

She stared at him a moment. "And who is going to help me?"

"I will." He jabbed his chest with his thumb for emphasis. "I've been known to be pretty handy with a feather duster."

She laughed. "My goodness. Can you do dishes too?"

"When I have to." He smiled and leaned toward her. "What do you say? I think it's a fine idea."

Before either of them could comment, Ichiko brought their orders. "Here you are." She put a plate of food in front of Rhys, then handed the bag to Goldie.

She paid for it, then turned to him. "This has been enlightening. Are there any other stories about the townspeople? Especially ones I should be warned about?"

He sighed. "Hoskins is fine. He wanted to find a way to a better life and went about it the wrong way."

"If he abducted someone, he broke the law, Rhys."

"And he did his time, paid his debt to society." He got to his feet to escort her to the door. "Don't think ill of him, Goldie. There are others in this town that have a past. Look at my mother."

"Your mother was defending herself. She wouldn't be charged for murder." Goldie looked away.

He knew what she was thinking. "And neither will you. The judge will be through in a couple of weeks, though, and he might want to question you."

"I'd like to know what happened to the other passengers. Would he want question them too?"

"If any of them are still in town, yes." He wasn't sure what else to say. He didn't want her fretting over it. "You handled yourself admirably, Goldie. I'm proud of you."

She stared at him. "Rhys, you don't know me. I could be another Hoskins."

"But you're not. Are you?"

"What if I was?"

"Stay here long enough and you'll find redemption. It happens a lot in this town. Remind me to introduce you to Nellie Davis. Better yet, her daughter Charlotte. She's married to Matthew Quinn down at the mercantile."

She looked at the bag in her hands, then the door. "Perhaps another time, I'd better get back. Connie and Hoskins are waiting for their lunch."

"Did they buy you a sandwich?"

"They did. And… well, I like Hoskins. He's a little odd, and acts like a head butler. But I've enjoyed his company. Connie's too."

Rhys smiled. "It's nice to see the three of you are on a first-name basis now."

She shrugged. "Well, like you said, no one really stands on ceremony in this town. I've noticed everyone's on a first-name basis."

He gave her a warm smile. "As it should be." He opened the door for her. "I'm going to practice some shooting later. You wouldn't happen to know if Hoskins owns a gun, would you?"

Her eyes lit up. "Shooting?"

"Yes, and I'm trying to find someone to practice with."

"You don't know how to shoot?" Her cheeks went pink.

"I could be better. Why?"

She shook her head. "Nothing. It's good that you want some practice. But I don't know if Hoskins is such a good choice."

"Well, perhaps I'll stop by the hotel on my way back to the bank and ask him." He'd also like another chance to speak with Goldie.

"Fine, I'll mention you want to practice. But maybe you should talk to Connie instead."

He laughed. "What for?"

"Because I've seen a rifle in her room. And I don't think it belongs to Hoskins."

He laughed some more. "I have no doubt she owns it, nor would she hesitate to use it if she had to. Thank goodness there's never been a need."

Her face was etched with worry. "Do you think there will be?"

He stepped closer. "It never hurts to be prepared. In the meantime, try not to think about it."

"Is that why you want to practice? So you're prepared?" She glanced at the door.

"Goldie, everything's going to be fine, understand? There are no outlaws, no one's trying to rob the bank, no one's coming here to cause trouble."

She swallowed. "How do you know?"

He sighed. "I don't, honey, but this is Nowhere. And nothing much ever happens here."

She nodded. "I'll practice with you."

He took a step back. "What?"

"I'll borrow Connie's rifle. In fact, I have my own pistol."

11

When Goldie returned to the hotel, Connie and Hoskins were seated at the kitchen table waiting for lunch. "What took you so long?" Connie asked.

Goldie set the bag on the table. "I ran into Rhys Miller and had a small chat. But only until the sandwiches were ready."

"Come now, dear," Hoskins said. "It is lunchtime, after all. You can't expect the girl to go to Hank's and come back quickly."

Connie opened the bag and took out the wrapped sandwiches, giving one to Hoskins. "Fine. I apologize, dear. I guess I'm just a little nervous about everything going on."

Goldie took a seat. "What do you mean? What's happening?"

"Well, Samijo and Charity came to town then rushed back on the afternoon train."

Goldie had to think. Hoskins told her just yesterday that the train came through town twice a day, several times a week. "I don't understand. What's the problem?"

"The problem, my dear," Hoskins said, "is that some of their farmhands saw strangers lurking about."

Goldie stopped breathing. "Strangers?"

"Don't pay him no mind," Connie said. "He told me, and I've been nervous as a cat ever since." She narrowed her eyes at her husband.

He unwrapped his sandwich. "I thought you ought to know. So we can take precautions as needed."

Goldie gulped. "You don't think it's the train robbers, do you?"

"Oh, now we've gone and done it," Connie said. "We've upset you. I'm sorry, dear." She patted Goldie's hand as she unwrapped a sandwich with the other.

Goldie stared at the ham and cheese, her heart in her throat. If it was the train robbers, then why would they be here? They weren't likely to rob the train at the station. There could be only one reason and she knew what it was. She closed her eyes and winced.

"Now don't think something bad is going to happen," Hoskins urged. "Having had a, shall we say, colorful past, most outlaws will try to get as far away from the scene of the crime as they can."

Connie eyed him. "The smart ones."

"Connie," he huffed. "That's not fair."

"Let's not talk about that now." She patted Goldie's hand again. "Now don't you fret. Just because my nerves are on edge doesn't mean yours have to be too."

"She's right," Hoskins said. "One fidgety female in the place is enough."

Connie slapped him with her napkin. "Will you be quiet?"

"Can I borrow your rifle?"

They looked at her like she'd grown a third eye. "What was that?" Connie asked.

Goldie gave them an imploring look. "Your rifle? I've seen it in your parlor, Connie. May I borrow it?"

"Oh, now wait a minute." Hoskins waved a hand at her.

"You don't need to be handling a firearm, young lady. Especially when you don't know…"

"I can shoot."

They stared at her again. "What was that, dear?" Connie asked.

Goldie nodded. "You heard me. I can shoot."

"Oh, dear me." Connie glanced at Hoskins and back. "You can? Who taught you?"

"My father. He was a Texas Ranger at one time and a crack shot." She looked at her sandwich. "Shouldn't someone say the blessing?"

Connie quickly bowed her head. "Dear Lord, for what we are about to receive, may we be truly thankful. Amen." She looked at Goldie. "A Texas Ranger?"

Goldie nodded and began to eat. Either they were going to loan her the rifle or not. If they didn't, she could use the pink pistol. She was better with a rifle and hadn't handled a pistol in a while. If that was all she had, then Goldie wanted to make sure she was still as good as she used to be.

"Well, well," Hoskins drawled. "You can shoot, eh?"

"Rhys Miller was going to practice this afternoon, and I told him I'd go with him." There, it was out. They could think what they wanted.

"Rhys?" Connie drummed her fingers on the tabletop. "I know he's shot before. He's done target practice with the Weavers at the harvest. But that was years ago." She looked at Hoskins. "What do you think, dear?"

He looked between them and shrugged. "Loan her the rifle. And I'll see what she can do."

"You?" Goldie said. "Don't tell me you're planning on coming along?"

"And what's wrong with that? It is our rifle after all. You said you can handle a gun, but I'd like to see it for myself."

She fought against a sigh. It wouldn't do to be rude. "Very

well. Then I'll see what *you* can do." She smiled and took a generous bite of her sandwich.

He nodded in return and started to eat. Connie, thank goodness, said nothing. This was unusual for her, and Goldie wondered if she'd go on a rant later. The other day she talked nonstop about the price of dried beans and coffee and almost drove Goldie and Hoskins around the bend. Hoskins, used to his wife's idiosyncrasies, sent Connie down to the mercantile so she could complain to the Quinns. Goldie hoped Betsy was taking a nap at the time so her son and daughter-in-law could deal with her instead.

When lunch was over, she got back to work stripping beds and doing laundry. Connie told her that people didn't pass through and stay as often as they use to. Goldie figured it was because there was nothing here of interest. She was wrong. Both Connie and Hoskins told her about Bella Weaver's creations. Samijo and Charity (she was married to Arlan's other brother, Benjamin) had brought a batch of dresses to town for Quinn's Mercantile. Goldie promised herself she'd look at them when she had the time, but couldn't buy one. She didn't have the money. She wished she did.

As she washed the sheets, she thought about the Weaver farm and its harvest. Hoskins said it was a grand time, and that he and Connie had taken part over the years ever since he came to town. She wasn't about to mention that Rhys told her his past even if it was common knowledge. After all, he didn't have to work with the rest of town. But he did have to work with her.

By the time she finished, there was a small window of opportunity to get in some target practice before she had to help with dinner. She found Connie in the kitchen washing some lettuce from the garden. "May I borrow the rifle now?"

Connie fidgeted. "Very well, but be sure Hoskins goes with you. And for Heaven's sake, don't let him shoot himself in the foot. He says he can handle a gun, but I haven't seen him do it."

Goldie bit her lip. This could be interesting. "Do you have ammunition?"

"Yes, Hoskins will show you where it is. Do you know how to load it?"

She smiled. "I do." She sauntered out of the kitchen and headed for the parlor. When she entered, Hoskins was already there. "Are you ready? We have some time before dinner."

He patted the firearm at his side. "Sure am." He picked up the rifle, put a box of bullets in his jacket pocket and grinned. "Shall we see if Rhys is ready?"

She smiled as excitement crept up her spine. This was going to be fun. "Of course."

He looked at the valise in her hand. "What's that?"

"My pistol. I don't have a gun belt."

His eyebrows shot up, and he smiled. "You should get one."

They left the hotel and headed for the bank. Luckily for them, Rhys was just coming out the door. It wouldn't do to walk in carrying guns and a rifle. Then again, this was Nowhere, so maybe no one would think anything of it.

"Hoskins," Rhys said. "Why are you carrying that rifle?"

Hoskins stood proudly and patted the gun at his side. "I'm wearing my handy revolver and this rifle because we're going shooting."

Rhys's eyes lit up. "Wonderful—it will be nice to have you along. I suppose you already heard from Goldie that she can shoot."

"I did. Poor Connie's fit to be tied but I do like to do a little practice now and then."

"Glad to hear it," Rhys said. "We'll stop by my place so I can get my gun."

"I didn't know you owned a firearm," Hoskins said.

"I borrowed one from Spencer." He put a hand in his

pocket and pulled out a deputy's star. "See, I've been officially deputized."

Hoskins fixed his eyes on it. "Is that so?"

Rhys eyed him. "Don't tell me you'd like to be deputized too?"

"Why not?" Hoskins beamed. "Not that anything will happen, but it might be fun to say I was a lawman for a short time."

"Yes," Rhys agreed. "But you realize that if something happens, you'll be called on to do what's necessary to protect the town."

"Of course, of course," Hoskins said. "Now let's be off, we're wasting daylight."

Goldie trailed behind the two men as they talked about firearms and started telling stories. Rhys didn't mention her valise, and she hoped she didn't embarrass them. How were they going to deal with the fact she was a better shot? Then again, she might be wrong, and they were both well versed in using pistols and rifles.

She waited on the porch with Hoskins while Rhys went inside to retrieve his weapon. When he came out, they set off down the road about twenty minutes until they reached an enormous field. There was no livestock in it, no crops planted—it was just a grazing pasture. "Who does this belong to?" Goldie asked.

"We're at the edge of Warren Johnson's property," Rhys said. "People come here to shoot now and then so he won't mind." He pointed to an old wooden fence that had a few cans and bottles sitting on the top rail. "See?"

She nodded, smiled, then looked around for anything else that they might use for targets. "You didn't bring something to shoot at?"

The two men looked at each other and shrugged.

Goldie bit her lip again. "No matter. I suppose we can reuse the cans."

Hoskins laughed. "As you can see, whoever practiced here before left their targets."

"Only because they didn't hit them," Rhys said with a laugh. "Let's hope they aren't still there when we're done."

She raised her eyebrows and smiled. "Yes, let us hope. Now, who wants to go first?"

"I'll give it a go," Hoskins said happily. He un-holstered his pistol, then took a few steps forward. "How many paces do you think that is?"

"I'd say about twenty yards," she said.

Rhys looked at her, then the bottles and cans in the distance. "I think you're right."

She arched an eyebrow but said nothing. Instead, she gave Hoskins a nod for him to proceed.

He stepped forward, cocked his gun, and took aim. When he fired, Rhys jumped. She didn't.

Rhys stared at her. "You didn't even flinch."

"Well, I have had some experience with guns."

"Goldie told us her father was a retired Texas Ranger. Isn't that something?" Hoskins took aim again and fired. Nothing. He shook his head. "I wonder if there's something wrong with my gun."

"Somehow I don't think so," Rhys said. "Shall I try?"

Goldie stood, her hands clasped behind her back. "Go right ahead."

He gave her a smile cocked his gun, took aim, and fired. Nothing. "Drat."

Hoskins slapped him on the back. "Don't feel bad, my boy. You're in good company." He chuckled. "Seems were both lousy shots."

Rhys took a deep breath and tried again. This time he managed to hit the fence. A small piece of wood flew off and landed on the ground. Unfortunately, it was the fence post farthest from the targets. Rhys shook his head. "I'm more out of practice than I thought."

"May I try?" Goldie asked."

"Of course, my dear." Hoskins reached for the rifle he'd set on the ground. "You know how to work this?"

"I do." She looked it over. "This is a Smith & Wesson revolving rifle. My father owned one. Bullets?"

Hoskins handed her a few. She loaded the rifle, cocked it, and took aim. She fired in rapid succession. Bottles shattered and cans flew off the fence rail. Done, she tucked the rifle under one arm and smiled at the men. "That wasn't so bad considering how long it's been. Now I'll try my pistol."

Rhys and Hoskins openly gawked. "Not bad?" Rhys said. "That was incredible!" He looked at his firearm, then at Hoskins. "Looks like we need more practice than we thought."

12

Rhys didn't know what to make of the blond beauty with the rifle. She didn't flinch, didn't waver, only aimed and fired. Good grief, what a shot! Part of him was jealous while the rest of him was in awe. "Your father taught you?"

"Yes." She loaded her pistol. It had a pink handle, and he wondered where she got it. "Too bad his talent with a gun couldn't save him."

He took a step closer. "I beg your pardon?"

She glanced at the targets. "My parents died in a house fire. I was out with friends at the time and was late getting home. We went to a play."

His eyes flicked to Hoskins and back. Judging from the look on his face, this was the first he'd heard of it. "I'm sorry to hear that."

"You mother didn't tell you?" she asked.

"No. Mother tends to keep other people's business to herself."

She raised her eyebrows at Hoskins but said nothing. Connie was the opposite and everyone in town knew it. "It's the reason I became a mail-order bride. With my parents gone, it was difficult for me to survive on my own."

"Well, you needn't worry about that now," Hoskins said jovially. "And considering what an excellent shot you are, well, I must say I feel safer having you at the hotel."

She smiled then handed him the rifle. "Would you like to try this?"

"Don't mind if I do." He took the rifle from her and took aim. "Oh, wait a minute, we need to reset the cans. You hit every one." He laughed, handed the rifle to Rhys, then headed for the fence.

Goldie watched him go, then fixed her eyes on the grassy ground. Rhys was bound to ask questions about her parents. She didn't want to talk about them. It was a painful memory that still haunted her even a year later. She thought enough time had passed but it hadn't. Still, she couldn't avoid the topic forever, especially not with someone as perceptive as Rhys. She took a deep breath and turned to him. "I'm sorry if I sounded rude earlier. It's just hard for me to talk about my parents."

Rhys nodded in understanding. "I can only imagine. But if you ever feel like talking, I'm here to listen."

Goldie smiled gratefully. She felt a warmth in her chest that she hadn't in a long time. It was strange, but being around Rhys made her feel safe and cared for. She knew it was foolish to entertain such thoughts. After all, he was practically a stranger to her. Still, a part of her wondered what it would be like to be with someone like him. Someone who was kind and gentle, yet strong and brave. So what if he couldn't shoot?

As if reading her thoughts, Rhys cleared his throat. "I was hoping you could show me how you hit those targets. It was like it was no trouble at all."

Goldie perked up at the idea. "Well, that's what a lot of practice does. I'd be happy to teach you."

Rhys grinned. "Great. When can we start?"

Goldie tried to ignore the flutter in her heart. She didn't know what the future held, but she knew one thing for sure. She was going to enjoy teaching Rhys how to shoot straight. "I'll have to see if I have any free time this week."

He smiled. "We're going out to the Weavers' on Friday. Remember what I said about getting your work done in half the time if you had help." He looked at Hoskins who was carefully placing the tin cans on the fence. "We can talk to Hoskins when he comes back."

She gazed at the ground again. "But I don't know them well yet and…"

"I do," he blurted.

She noted the excitement on his face. "You're really looking forward to my teaching you?"

"Yes. You're fantastic. And I admit, I've never known a woman who was good with a gun. Except Annie Oakley, but who can compare with her?"

She bit her lip as she looked at the pistol in her hand. Forget about the rifle, she should practice with this. But doggone if her competitive spirit didn't get the best of her. "You're right, she is the best."

As they continued to talk, Goldie noticed a shift in Rhys's demeanor. He seemed more guarded, almost as if he was unsure of something. She wanted to ask him what was wrong, but she didn't want to pry. Instead, she tried to keep the conversation light, and before she knew it, they were laughing about something silly Hoskins did at the hotel the other day.

But even as they laughed and joked, she couldn't help but study Rhys. There was something about him that drew her in, something that made her want to know him better. She couldn't quite put her finger on it, but whatever it was, it was powerful. It made her think of Theodore and his father. They were strangers to her, but the loss was devastating, and, like Mrs. Miller said, made more so by the loss of her dreams. Did she dare allow herself to get close to Rhys?

They shot a few more rounds then headed back. Hoskins and Rhys kept complimenting her on her fine aim and both wanted lessons. She hoped what she discerned earlier in Rhys wasn't jealousy. But even so, it was gone now.

As they walked and Rhys and Hoskins chatted about one of the local farmers, Goldie couldn't shake off the feeling that Rhys differed from the other men she'd met. He was charming and kind, but there was something else about him that made her curious. Maybe it was the way he looked at her, like she was the only person in the world that mattered. Or maybe it was how he laughed at her jokes, even the ones that weren't funny. Whatever it was, she found herself wanting to spend more time with him.

As they approached Rhys' house, he talked about his life and the adventures he'd had in and around Nowhere. Goldie listened intently, hanging on his every word. She'd never imagined small-town life before and was surprised at the amount of things people did to entertain themselves, from dances to barn raisings, fishing, horse races, and some good old-fashioned pranks. The thought of staying in a place like Nowhere was both exciting and terrifying. But she still faced the same problem. How was she going to live?

When they reached the hotel, Rhys turned to her. "Thank you for practicing with me today. I had a great time."

Goldie smiled. "You're welcome. I had fun too."

"So did I!" Hoskins said. "Wait until I tell Connie. She won't believe it!" He took the rifle from Goldie and hurried inside.

Rhys hesitated for a moment before speaking again. "I was wondering if you'd like to have dinner with my family and me tonight. Mother is trying her hand at a new recipe she got from Leona Riley."

Goldie's heart skipped a beat. "I'd like that, if I can get away. What time?"

"Six o'clock?"

Goldie nodded. "I'll have to let Connie and Hoskins know."

He smiled and nodded at the hotel doors. "I think Hoskins is growing fond of you."

She blushed. "Perhaps. And you were right. Despite what you told me about his past, I can see he's not the man he was years ago. From the sounds of it, he tried to be bad and failed at it."

Rhys laughed. "That sums it up." He looked at her and said nothing for a moment.

She returned his gaze, her heart skipping again. "I should go inside."

"I'll come fetch you at six."

She nodded. "That would be fine."

He tipped his hat and, with a parting smile, was off.

As he walked away, a surge of excitement struck. Mercy, she shouldn't feel this way, but there was no denying the pounding of her heart or the tiny tingles of excitement coursing through her. For crying out loud, it was only dinner. But she couldn't stop the fluttering in her stomach at the thought of spending time with Rhys and his family. She knew it was silly to get so worked up over a simple meal, but considering the way he looked at her just now, or the ease in which they talked… oh, doggone it, she found herself wanting more.

After telling Connie about Rhys' invitation, she spent the rest of the afternoon helping her with a few small chores to make up for not eating at the hotel. As soon as she finished, she went to change.

She had a cream-colored dress with a darker cream sash and lace that she'd worn to a New Year's Eve party last year and received a lot of compliments on. The soft ivory material accentuated her curves, and her mother hoped the dress would help her attract the eye of an eligible bachelor. It didn't. Everyone knew her father was an ex-Texas Ranger.

But tonight, Goldie didn't care about attracting any bachelor's attention. She wanted to spend some time with the Millers, maybe give Rhys a few pointers, then get back to the hotel before Connie and Hoskins started to think she didn't need her job at the hotel. She wanted to take a good look around and make sure they did.

In her room she brushed her hair until it shone, put it up, then slipped on her dress. After studying her reflection in the mirror, she took a deep breath and headed out the door.

Rhys was waiting for her outside the hotel, dressed in what looked like his Sunday best. He was handsome in his black suit and white shirt, and it was all she could do not to outright stare. *Don't even think about it… yes, he's handsome, but also probably a little put out that you could out-shoot him.*

"You look lovely." His eyes roamed over her, and he coughed into his hand. "Excuse me."

Goldie blushed. If she didn't know any better, she'd say he was nervous. Well, that made two of them.

He offered his arm, and they headed to his house. As they walked, her stomach fluttered, but it wasn't because she was on the arm of a handsome man—she was more nervous than she thought. In a blink of an eye, she'd lost everything, including a chance at love. She shouldn't think of Rhys as a prospect; he wasn't. What he was, was impressed with her shooting, and this wasn't the first time she'd received an invitation because of her ability to handle a gun.

When they arrived at his house, Mrs. Miller greeted her warmly. The house was just as cozy and inviting as ever. *Don't get used to this.* She'd have to keep telling herself that. There were no guarantees out here and she was hanging by a thread. Things could change in an instant, and had when the robbers boarded the train.

They sat down to dinner, and Goldie was blissfully distracted by Mrs. Miller's cooking. Her new recipe, a chicken dish with a cream sauce, was delicious, and she wondered if Connie would like it. She smiled as she pictured Connie and

Hoskins arguing with each other in the kitchen over the ingredients.

As they ate, they talked and laughed, and Goldie found herself relaxing more and more. After dinner, Rhys suggested they play a game of cards, and everyone eagerly agreed. She loved playing cards, and was surprised at how much fun she was having with Rhys and his family. She even found herself forgetting about her worries for a little while.

As the night wore on, Goldie noticed the way Rhys looked at her, his eyes lingering a little longer than necessary. She knew she was being silly, but she couldn't help the way she felt.

After their game, Rhys offered to walk her back to the hotel.

"Is it time to go already?" Goldie heard the disappointment in her voice and hoped no one else noticed.

"I had a wonderful time tonight," Rhys said, smiling.

"I must say," Mrs. Miller said, "so did I. Goldie, you'll have to join us again." She began to clear the dessert dishes.

"Thank you for inviting me. This was lovely." Too lovely, as a matter of fact. She could get used to this but didn't dare. If she wanted to survive, she'd have to move on, no matter how nice the people here were. They might not be so nice if she couldn't come up with a way to support herself.

Rhys stood and went behind her chair. "Shall we go?"

Goldie took one last look around the homey dining room and swallowed hard. If she was smart, she wouldn't do this again. "Yes. Let's."

13

Several days went by and the whole town was talking about Goldie's proficiency with a gun. But they didn't hear it from Connie—they heard it from Hoskins. "You should have seen her!" he'd say to anyone who would listen. "I've never seen anything like it!"

Standing off to one side, she'd roll her eyes or slink into a corner so she wouldn't have to talk to anyone. Half the towns-people probably didn't believe him. She hoped he wouldn't have to set up targets for her to shoot off the fence rail just so he could prove he was right. Wouldn't that be something? Half the town lined up behind her to watch her shoot?

She cut up some potatoes and tried to think of something else. Naturally the only other thing her mind would go to was Rhys. She closed her eyes, took a deep breath, and willed his face to vamoose. It didn't.

"Are you not feeling well?" Connie asked as she came into the kitchen.

"I'm fine."

"Glad to hear it, because Hoskins and I have decided to go to the Weaver farm and help with the harvest this weekend."

She looked up from her work. "This weekend?"

"Yes, and we'd like to know if you want to come along."

"But that would leave no one to man the hotel."

She stood on the other side of the worktable. "I made an arrangement with Charlotte Quinn from the mercantile. She'll look after things while we're gone."

Her heart sped up at the thought of taking the train to the Weavers, even though part of her didn't give a whit if she never stepped foot on another train again. "Thank you for thinking of me."

"You've done well here, Goldie." Connie smiled. "Thank you for your hard work."

She gulped. Was she about to tell her they no longer needed her?

"Hoskins and I are impressed," Connie continued. "And your cooking isn't bad either."

"But?"

"No but, dear. I was giving you a compliment." She looked at the potatoes. "Finish those. I'm going to check the chicken."

Goldie watched her open the oven and poke at the bird. She had to stop thinking the world was about to fall apart. But her little corner was all she had, and she feared that was exactly what could happen. It had happened before—those darn train robbers saw to that.

Goldie's eyes flicked to the ceiling. She should practice with the pink pistol. She could carry it and use it for protection. It was less conspicuous than a rifle and, though she wasn't as good with a pistol, it would do the trick.

She set the potatoes on the stove to boil, then went to the garden behind the hotel to pick some vegetables. She'd never had a garden before and like spending time in Connie and Hoskins'. She didn't know what it was about weeding and picking vegetables or herbs, but there was a satisfaction to it.

She'd taken food for granted until after the fire. Father had always provided for them and was in no hurry to see his daughter wed. At twenty, she was getting nervous about finding a husband. In another couple of years most folks in Kansas City would consider her a spinster. What did they think here?

She returned to the kitchen and washed the lettuce and tomatoes she'd picked. She'd make a salad to go with their roast chicken and potatoes, then put a batch of cookies in the oven for dessert. One thing she liked about Connie and Hoskins, they always set a splendid table. Seems Hoskins' years as a head butler ingrained some good things into him. He was in the dining room even now, whistling a merry tune as he set the table for the evening meal.

Goldie smiled. They were like an aunt and uncle she didn't meet until she was older. Yesterday she caught herself imagining she was visiting them for the summer.

But the fact was, she had no one. Her parents had been her only living relatives, and what few friends she had had little to do with her once they found out she had nothing. Her parents were probably the most affluent among her peers. Funny how you were judged by the amount of money you had, even among the lower middle class.

"Woolgathering, dear?" Connie said.

Goldie blinked a few times. "I suppose so."

"Start thinking about packing a few things to take to the Weavers. You'll stay with one of the families. We always do. If you're lucky, it will be Calvin and Bella. Land sakes, that woman can cook."

She smiled at the excitement in Connie's eyes. "I'm looking forward to it." Part of her was still loath to set foot on the train, but who knew if she'd ever get another chance to see the famous Weaver farm?

When it was time for dinner, Hoskins could barely contain his own enthusiasm. "I'm telling you, we should have a contest." He took a bite of chicken, then waved his fork at her as he chewed and swallowed. "Just think, you could out-shoot every man there!"

Connie looked at Goldie and shook her head. "Really, dear, don't listen to him." She gave Hoskins a flat look. "Before you know it, he'll be selling tickets."

His eyes lit up. "Hey, that's a great idea!"

"Hoskins!"

Goldie snorted with laughter. Yes, the two were growing on her and she was going to have to be careful lest she become too attached. It was hard enough being around Rhys. In fact, she did her best to avoid him the last few days and wondered if he thought she was being standoffish. But she didn't like the fuss the men were making about her shooting. Anyone could learn, including women. She was proof of that.

When the meal was over, she helped clear away the dishes, then made her cookies. Connie and Hoskins retired to the parlor to play a game of cribbage and she enjoyed listening to them bicker about the score. If Hoskins could get away with cheating, he would. But only because Connie beat him almost every game.

As Goldie waited for the cookies to bake, she prepared a tray with cups, saucers, cream and sugar. The three had fallen into a routine since her arrival, and now that they knew where each of them stood in their little arrangement, she was more comfortable and so were they.

The cookies done, she put some on a plate, filled each cup, then carried everything into the parlor.

"There you are, my dear," Connie said. "You know, we're going to be terribly spoiled."

"We already are," Hoskins said with a wink. "I must admit, it's nice having you around, Goldie. I'm truly sorry about what happened to Theodore and Ben. I never met them, but Connie's talked about them now and then."

Goldie nodded. "Thank you. I guess we never know what the world is going to serve us."

Connie's smile was heartfelt. "You didn't deserve what you got, and neither did Ben and Teddy. I hope the law is doing something about those no-good outlaws. They need to be behind bars, the lot of them." She reached for the cup and saucer Goldie offered. "Thank you, dear."

Goldie gave one to Hoskins, took one for herself, then sat on the other side of the parlor. "What's it going to be like at the Weaver farm?"

"Oh, my," Hoskins said. "It's wonderful. But of course we think so—we're not there for weeks on end harvesting all those apples, pears and whatever else they grow out there."

"You must see Mary's sewing room," Connie said. "It's incredible."

Goldie closed her eyes and took a sip of coffee. A sudden pang of loneliness hit, and she wondered what it would be like to live on a vast farm with dozens of other people. Especially if most of them were family.

Family. She no longer had one.

She watched Connie and Hoskins as they started another game of cribbage. Such an odd pair, yet they fit together perfectly. Would she and Theodore have fit, or would they have been at odds with one another? Her parents fit. In fact, Mother and Father were a perfect fit. They did everything together almost since the day they met. They even died together.

She closed her eyes against the tears that threatened. If she hoped to make a life for herself, she didn't think she could do it here. Nowhere wasn't big enough, and there was no one…

"Goldie, dear, is something wrong?"

She met Connie's concerned gaze and shook her head. "No, not at all." She eyed the cribbage board. Her parents loved the game. "I think I'll turn in. But first, I'll sit outside."

"That's fine, dear," Connie said. "But do be careful."

A shudder coursed through her. Her time with the train robbers had a lasting effect, and she thought to ask Mrs.

Miller how long it took before she stopped having bad dreams.

Outside she headed up and across the street to the sheriff's office. Deputy McKay was on duty, and she'd be safe enough sitting on the bench by his door. It was just past the window, so he might not see her, but that was okay. She'd be safe and could have her privacy at the same time.

When she reached the bench, she eased onto it with a sigh. How did her life become this? First her parents, then Theodore and his father. What next? At this point she was better off alone. Just when something good happened, something else did to erase it. What if she stayed, met a man and got married? How long before something happened to him? Things could happen to you anywhere. Even in a silly little town called Nowhere.

"Goldie?"

She looked to find Rhys standing in the doorway to the sheriff's office. "What are you doing here?"

"I might ask you the same." She tried to look past him to see if the deputy was standing nearby. He wasn't.

Rhys closed the door, went to the bench and sat. "Did you take a stroll? You shouldn't be out here alone."

"I'm not." She sat back. "You're here."

He gave her a hint of a smile. "Only because I had some business to discuss with Ollie McKay."

She clasped her hands in her lap. "I just wanted some air before going to bed."

"It's a fine night for that." He crossed his arms and leaned back.

"Indeed, it is." The night sky was full of brilliant stars. She knew because she stopped in the middle of the street to look at them before continuing to the bench.

"How long have you been out here?" he asked.

"Not long. A few minutes."

"Would you rather I left you alone? Though I'll be honest, I'm not keen on the idea."

Her chest warmed. Was he trying to protect her? "I don't mind some company."

He settled himself more comfortably. "Good, because I'm staying."

She smiled. "Somehow I doubt a band of outlaws is going to charge through town, grab me from the front of a sheriff's office, then ride off."

"Stranger things have happened."

She laughed. "Where?"

Now he laughed. "Clear Creek."

"You keep bringing that place up. Why? Is it that bad? Have you ever been there?"

"Me? No, but a lot of the Weavers have, and some of them married into the Cooke family and vice versa."

"Cooke? Who are they?"

"They own the Triple-C Ranch just outside Clear Creek. That town is smaller than this one but sees far more action than we do. Things… happen there."

"Well, that has nothing to do with me."

He glanced at her, and she noted how handsome he was even in the dim light. "Maybe so," he said. "But my point is, if outlaws riding through town abducting women can happen there, then it can just as easily happen here."

She straightened. "Did that really happen?"

He turned to face her. "It did. Which is why I'll be escorting you back across the street. Just as soon as you're ready."

She half-smiled. He *was* protecting her. *No, don't even think about it. You know something bad will happen. Then he'll be gone just like Mother and Father and Theodore. You never even got the chance to get to know him!*

"Goldie," he said softly. "I hope I didn't upset you."

She looked into his eyes and was thankful for the darkness.

It kept him from seeing her tears. "No, you didn't." She stood. "I'd like to go back now."

He left the bench, looked at her and smiled. "Then I'll take you home."

Together they left the bench and crossed the street to the hotel. With each step, Goldie fought the icy ball of fear growing in her gut. The kind that told her she was better off alone.

14

Friday afternoon, Goldie, Connie, and Hoskins boarded the train with the Miller family. "I always look forward to this," Mr. Miller said, taking a seat next to his wife.

Goldie took the seat behind them. She'd packed the pistol, a change of clothes and remembered Connie asking her if she had a bathing costume when they were about to leave the hotel. She sighed as her eyes darted to her valise at her feet. Her parents used to take her swimming at a lake not far from the city. Those were good times, and she did her best to keep the tears at bay.

"No matter," Connie had said. "I'm sure you can borrow one from one of the Weaver women."

She looked out the window as the train whistle blew and wondered if Connie had packed a bathing costume. Apparently sorting fruit was hard work, and the Weavers and whatever help they had went to the creek that ran through the property to cool off before dinner. After they ate, everyone did another round of sorting for a couple of hours before turning in. Hmm, how many other folks from town were at the farm? She'd have to wait until they arrived to find out.

Rhys spoke to the conductor, then took the seat across the aisle from hers. Just as he sat, the whistle blew again, and the train pulled out of the station. "I'm looking forward to this," he said with a smile. "I can't wait to show you around the farm."

She smiled back. "I admit, my curiosity is piqued. I've noticed the way people talk about the place whenever it comes up in conversation."

"The Weavers have built themselves a prosperous operation," Mr. Miller said. "As a widow with four sons, Mary Weaver did what most women wouldn't think of in her situation. She kept going."

"Yes," Mrs. Miller said. "And when those boys got a little older and married, the farm grew into what it is today."

Goldie nodded as the train chugged along. As much as she was looking forward to finally getting to see firsthand what everyone kept talking about, she couldn't shake the feeling of unease that nagged her. Ever since hearing about those strangers lurking around the farm, she'd had a case of the jitters. What if it *was* the train robbers?

She tried to think of anything else and wished she'd thought to bring a book as Rhys had. He opened it and quietly read. Part of her wouldn't mind starting a conversation with him, but she didn't want to interrupt his reading.

Just as well. She dozed off and was surprised when she didn't wake until they were almost to their destination. When she did, Rhys was sitting, his feet in the aisle, a smile on his face. "Have a nice nap?"

She blinked back sleep. "What? Oh, I suppose." She rubbed her eyes and looked around. There were apple orchards on both sides of the tracks. "We're almost there," she said to no one in particular.

"That we are." Rhys peered out the windows on her side of the train car. "We'll get settled, help out where we can until the break before dinner, then I'll try to show you around."

"Thank you. That would be nice." Goldie continued to watch out the window until the train pulled into the tiny station. She gathered her things, then followed the others onto the platform. She scanned the area, noted the stacked crates of apples waiting to be loaded onto the train, then spotted Arlan Weaver giving instructions to whom she guessed were farmhands. They began loading crates as Arlan waved at her. Connie and Hoskins headed straight for him, leaving Goldie to bring up the rear.

Rhys joined her. "Are you all right?"

She thought a moment. Was she? It wasn't far from here where her life had changed forever. She took a shuddering breath. "Yes, I'm fine."

"Miss Colson!" Arlan said as he approached. "It's good to see ya here."

She smiled even as a chill went up her spine. "Thank you, I'm looking forward to helping."

Arlan's hands went to his hips. "Did anyone tell ya how sore you'll get or warn ya about the heat?" He pulled a handkerchief from his pocket and wiped his brow.

"Well, no," she admitted.

He smiled. "Trust me, everyone'll be askin'." He offered his hand to Rhys.

Rhys shook it with a smile, spoke to Arlan briefly, then the group headed for the main farmhouse. A trail wound through trees, grassy patches, and a few stray apple trees laden with fruit, until it spilled into a backyard.

"Is that the main house?" Goldie asked.

"No, that's my brother Calvin's house," Arlan said. "The main farmhouse is next to the sortin' barn and the larger barn we use for our powdered milk production."

Goldie studied the house and barn in front of them, then the surrounding landscape. The Weaver farm was even more impressive than she'd imagined. The fields were vast and lush, and the farmhouse was a two-story building with a wraparound porch. As they walked, she noticed there were quite a few people from town already here. Some had tents set up near the barn and there were a couple in what had to be the front yard.

They kept going; the trail turning into a small lane. It wasn't long before the main house came into view. Like the previous house, it was two-storied with a wraparound porch, but this one was much bigger.

Goldie stopped and stared, taking it all in. The barns were large and well-maintained, and she could see horses and cows grazing in a nearby field beyond one orchard. But the thing that struck her most was the little white chapel on the other side of the lane that ran between it and the main farmhouse's front yard. "This is so picturesque."

"It certainly is," Rhys drew in a lungful of air. "I love the smell of the orchards at harvest."

She smiled as Hoskins waved at someone. "Well, well, there's a familiar face," he said with his usual chuckle. "Selena, Phoebe! How are you?"

Goldie followed his gaze. Two young women were approaching from the main house. She didn't know which was which, but both were striking with dark hair and green eyes.

"The older one is Selena," Hoskins said beside her. "Phoebe is her younger sister. She doesn't talk much, but she's sweet."

Selena smiled warmly when they reached them. "Welcome to the Weaver farm. We're so glad you could make it."

Goldie smiled in greeting as Selena and Phoebe drew closer. "It's nice to meet you both. I'm Goldie Colson."

"Yes," Selena said. "Uncle Arlan told us all about you."

Goldie did her best to smile. Did that include every detail of the train robbery?

"I'm Selena, and this is my sister Phoebe." She motioned to the girl next to her. She looked to be about fourteen or fifteen.

Phoebe simply nodded, smiled shyly, then kept her eyes on the grass. Had she been through something too? She recalled

Hoskins telling her something about Phoebe but couldn't remember what.

Goldie studied them. Selena seemed confident and self-assured, while Phoebe's eyes darted around nervously. Goldie had a pang of empathy for her. She knew firsthand how trauma could leave you feeling vulnerable and unsure of yourself. She offered Phoebe a warm smile. "Thank you for having me. I'm looking forward to helping out."

"We're happy to have you," Selena said. "And you're just in time for the first round of sorting. But first let's get you settled." She greeted the Millers, then waved at the farmhouse. "Lucien, Billie, Rhys, you'll stay with Granny Mary and Grandpa Harlan."

Goldie leaned toward Rhys and asked quietly, "Who is Harlan again?"

"Mary's second husband," he whispered back. "She remarried around the same time her youngest son Daniel got hitched."

She nodded. How would she keep track of all these people? As they walked toward the main house, she recognized a few folks from town, but didn't know their names. Maybe someone would introduce her to them later.

Hoskins and Connie exchanged pleasantries with Selena as they approached the house. Goldie listened to them and saw an old woman and old man sitting in chairs on the porch, both with a glass of lemonade in their hands. Phoebe caught up to her, smiled shyly and murmured a soft greeting.

Goldie smiled back as Selena led everyone up the porch steps. "Granny Mary, Harlan, may I introduce Miss Goldie Colson?"

The old woman got to her feet and handed her glass to Selena. "Glad to have you here, child." Without warning, she pulled Goldie into a hug. "It's a terrible thing that happened, just terrible." She drew back and smiled. "But from what I've heard from Samijo, you'll pull through." She looked at the

Millers. "Rhys, it's been a spell. Glad to see you could make it."

"I wouldn't miss it for the world, Granny Mary." He gave her a big smile then sidestepped to put himself next to Goldie. "I'd like to show Miss Colson around later if I could."

"Sure, go right ahead." She turned to the old man. "Harlan, meet Miss Colson."

He smiled, got to his feet, and lifted his glass. "Lemonade?"

Goldie smiled back. "I'd love some."

He turned to the young women. "Selena, Phoebe, get these friendly folks some lemonade while we get acquainted with Miss Colson here."

The sisters left to get what he asked.

"Well, now, I hear you hail from Kansas City." He smiled again, and Goldie caught the sympathy in his eyes. At least he wasn't saying anything about the train robbery.

"That's right. I was born and raised there."

Harlan nodded. "City girl, huh? Well, you're in for a different kind of life around here. But it's a good life, and a simple one."

It also couldn't support her, not from what she'd seen so far, and it wouldn't be long before she'd have to move on to some place that would.

He gestured toward the house. "Why don't we sit down and have a chat? I'd love to hear more about your life in Kansas City."

Goldie smiled and followed him to the rocking chairs he and his wife had used. Granny Mary and Mr. and Mrs. Miller sat down on a nearby bench, while Rhys and Hoskins took a seat on the steps. It wasn't long before Selena and Phoebe brought glasses of lemonade and passed them out to everyone.

"Thank you," Goldie said, taking a sip. It was sweet and refreshing and she gazed at the chapel across the lane.

"So, Miss Colson," Harlan said, settling into his chair. "What brings you all the way out here?"

Goldie hesitated. She didn't want to get into the details of the robbery, but she couldn't very well avoid the question. "I was a mail-order bride. The Fergusons and I were heading to Seattle. Mr. Ferguson, my future father-law, had work waiting for him there at a sawmill. As did his son."

"Ah, I see. Well, we certainly appreciate you taking the time to be our extra hands. It's a busy time of year."

"It's my pleasure." Goldie took another sip of lemonade and glanced over at Phoebe, who was sitting next to Selena and listening intently to their conversation. She couldn't help but notice that Phoebe kept her eyes down for minutes at a time and wondered what she could do to make the girl feel more comfortable.

As if sensing her thoughts, Selena spoke up. "Phoebe, why don't you show Miss Colson to her room at our house?"

"I'll be staying with you?" Goldie said in surprise.

"Yes. I know you might want to rest a little before the sorting starts." Selena nodded at Phoebe.

Phoebe turned to Goldie. "The house is this way."

Goldie set her glass on the table between the rocking chairs and stood. Now was her chance to speak to Phoebe and find out what her story was. Maybe then she could forget about her own for a while.

15

As they left the main farmhouse, Goldie noticed how Phoebe's hands shook as she led her to the other house. Strangers either made her nervous or it was something else, and Goldie could guess what. Those doggone train robbers. If someone on the farm saw strangers lurking around, then Phoebe probably wasn't the only one around here that was worried.

As they walked, she struck up a conversation. "Mrs. Ferguson told me your sister was a mail-order bride."

Phoebe nodded, her eyes still on the ground.

"You're very quiet," Goldie remarked gently. "Is everything okay?"

Phoebe smiled momentarily, but she didn't respond. Instead, she picked up the pace.

When they reached the smaller farmhouse, she led Goldie up the porch steps and through the front door. There was a staircase to their left, and a parlor to the right that led into a dining room. Both were large rooms, and she remembered something mentioned about the size of Calvin and Bella Weaver's household. At the end of the hallway, there was a door to the right, and one to the left. One must lead to the kitchen.

"I'll introduce you to Ma." Phoebe headed down the hall.

Goldie followed, feeling the weight of the silence between them. She wondered if Phoebe would open up to her but didn't want to push too hard. For one, she wasn't going to be here long. Who knew when she would return to the farm?

As they entered the kitchen, Goldie was hit by a wave of warmth and the smell of fresh bread. A familiar looking dark-haired woman kneaded dough at a worktable in the middle of the kitchen. Nearby was a huge table with at least twelve chairs. Goodness, Calvin's family was large!

The woman, her sleeves rolled up to her elbows, smiled when she saw them, then wiped her hands on her apron. "Phoebe, thank you for bringing our guest." She smiled again. "And you must be Goldie. I remember when you passed through on the train a couple of weeks ago. Welcome to our home. I'm Calvin's wife, Bella." Her voice was sweet and welcoming with an Italian accent.

Goldie relaxed a little as her mouth watered at the smell of food. "Thank you, ma'am."

"Just Bella, please." She looked around. "You'll have to excuse the mess—I've been baking all morning and haven't got things cleaned up since lunch."

"Is that what smells so wonderful?"

"That would be my spaghetti sauce for dinner." She took a lid off a large pot on the stove and gave it a stir.

Goldie noted Phoebe had retreated to the far side of the room, but at least her eyes weren't downcast. Instead, she eyed the pot as Bella returned the lid. She must be hungry. Goldie wondered if Phoebe was always like this, or if it was because of the strangers that had been lurking around.

"Phoebe," Bella said. "Why don't you show our guest to her room?" She smiled at Goldie. "You can put your bag away, then come down for a snack if you'd like. The sorting will start soon."

"Thank you," Goldie said.

Phoebe left the kitchen without a word and retraced her steps to the front hall and staircase.

"I heard your sister married Alastair Weaver," Goldie said, taking another stab at conversation.

Phoebe smiled. "He's a good man. Selena is very happy."

Goldie smiled back as they climbed the stairs. She followed Phoebe down the hall to a room on the left, which turned out to be a bedroom with a cozy sitting room. The bedroom area had a comfortable-looking bed, a dresser, and a small writing desk by the window. The walls were papered a light blue dotted with tiny flowers, the furniture serviceable and polished. There was a fireplace on the far wall, and a few paintings hung here and there. It was a warm and inviting space, and Goldie couldn't help but feel at ease.

"This used to be two smaller bedrooms," Phoebe explained, then gestured for Goldie to sit on the settee. She took the chair opposite. "We decided to make this one of the official guest rooms as we have more empty bedrooms than anyone. Everyone stays with us when they come to visit."

Goldie could sense Phoebe was still nervous, but at least she was talking. "Empty?"

She shrugged. "Everyone got married, and some moved away. Mama's seven brothers and sisters all lived here at one time."

"Seven?" Goldie breathed. "Goodness, I seem to recall Connie Ferguson mention something about your mother's siblings." She rubbed her temple. "To tell you the truth, since I arrived in Nowhere, I don't know if I'm coming or going."

"On account of the train robbery?" Phoebe whispered.

Goldie stared at her a moment. She didn't want to talk about it, but if it would help ease Phoebe's nerves, she would. "Yes." Now *her* eyes were downcast.

When she finally looked up, Phoebe's gaze met hers for a moment, then she looked away. "I know what it's like to be scared," she mumbled. "I... I don't like strangers very much. Especially not after what happened with those train robbers."

Goldie nodded. "I understand. But you don't have to worry about them. I'm sure they're long gone by now." She hoped. "In fact, I'm glad I came to help you and your family with the apple sorting."

Phoebe's eyes flickered with gratitude, and Goldie could tell she was warming up to her. Still, she didn't like talking about what happened on the train and changed the subject. "So tell me about your sister. What's she like?"

Phoebe's face lit up at the mention of Selena. "Oh, she's wonderful. She's kind and clever. And brave too. She rescued me from the fire that killed our parents and left everything behind to come here and marry Alastair."

Goldie could only stare. "You lost your parents in a fire?"

Phoebe nodded.

"Me too."

Phoebe stared at her a moment. "I'm sorry."

"I'm sorry too, and for you." Goldie mustered up a warm smile and glanced around the room. Time to change the subject again. "It's lovely here. Thank you for letting me stay with you and your family." She faced her. "You know, you remind me of someone I used to know in Kansas City. She was shy too, but she had a heart of gold."

Phoebe blushed. "I do?"

"Yes, she was our neighbor. Martha was her name." She hadn't thought of Martha for a long time and smiled at the memory of her friend. "Martha married when she turned eighteen and moved away."

"She married?"

Goldie caught the hopeful tone in Phoebe's voice. "You want to get married one day, don't you?"

She blushed head to toe and nodded.

Goldie smiled at her again, then stood. "We should get going. I don't want to keep your mother waiting."

Phoebe nodded and they left the room.

Downstairs Bella was taking off her apron and pushing loose wisps of hair from her face. Just the sight of her made Goldie tired. Maybe this would be more work than she thought.

They left for the sorting barn, Bella leading the way. "How do you like Nowhere?" she asked as they walked.

"It's smaller than what I'm used to. But peaceful like this place." Goldie looked around at the fields and surrounding orchards. "This is beautiful."

Bella's face brightened. "Yes, it is. We love it here. It's a good life. We have everything we need."

Goldie couldn't argue with that.

They arrived at the sorting barn and the sight that greeted her was overwhelming. There were stacks upon stacks of apple crates, and people were already hard at work sorting them. She was introduced to a few of the workers, but their names went in one ear and out the other. They all seemed friendly enough, but she couldn't shake the feeling that something was off. Maybe she was nervous at the thought that train robbers might be sneaking around. But wouldn't they have moved on by now? Why stick around?

She gulped. She knew why.

Goldie took a shuddering breath as Bella led her to the middle of a long wooden shelf built into the wall that ran the length of the barn. Bushels of apples were at each worker's feet, with one on the shelf in front of them. Each bushel was being sorted into a crate containing a layer of straw, on the other side of each worker.

"Now all you have to do is check for bad bruising, worm holes, punctures, that sort of thing," Bella explained. "The good apples go into the crate with the straw, the bad ones go into the crate at your feet. We use those apples for cider and other things."

Goldie nodded and noted the place next to her was empty, even though it was set up with apples to be sorted. She wondered who she'd be next to when she spied Rhys heading her way.

He waved as he approached then came alongside. "Isn't this something? What do you think?"

Bella smiled at them. "I'll leave you to it." She gave Rhys a nod and hurried off.

Goldie looked around. "It's overwhelming, to say the least."

"That it is." He got to work. "Bella explained everything?"

"Yes." She was glad for his company and now had someone familiar to talk to. But as she sorted, her mind wandered back to the conversation with Phoebe. She couldn't help but feel sorry for the girl. Losing her parents in a fire, she could relate to all too well. But the way Phoebe looked at her, the way she blushed when they talked about marriage… it was obvious she knew little about men considering her age. Did she know anything at all?

She shook her head, trying to clear her thoughts. This was not the time or place to be thinking such things. She had a job to do, and she needed to focus. But as the afternoon wore on and Phoebe kept stealing glances at her, Goldie sensed her growing desire to help the young woman. She'd always been drawn to innocence, and Phoebe was the epitome of it.

"Good gracious, it's getting hot." Rhys pulled a handkerchief from his pocket and wiped his brow.

Goldie nodded. She was sweating and wondered how far it was to the creek. Now she knew why people kept bringing it up. She didn't have a swimming costume, but dipping her feet into some water would certainly help cool her off.

The longer they worked, the hotter it got, and she noticed Bella and a few other women had left, probably to start dinner.

"Everyone is going to the creek later," Rhys said, breaking into her thoughts. "Will you go?"

His voice held the same hopeful tone as Phoebe's. "Yes. Though I have nothing to swim in."

"You can wade, that will help." He looked around. "Do you need some water?" She nodded and Rhys raised his hand.

Goldie didn't know what it meant, then saw a young boy heading their way with a bucket. "Water?" the boy asked expectantly.

"Thank you, Alvin." He took the ladle in the bucket, scooped up some water and offered it to Goldie. She took it without question and drank greedily.

"Would you like another?" the boy asked.

"Thank you." She scooped up another ladleful and drank.

"Alvin graduated to water boy this year," Rhys informed her.

She smiled and realized the child had a British accent. "How old are you, Alvin?"

"I'm six. How old are you?"

She blushed. "Young men do not ask young ladies their age."

He cocked his head. "But you're not young. You're much older than I am."

Rhys snorted into his hand.

"Alvin!" a man at the other end of the barn called. He too had a British accent. "Get on with it."

"Who is that?" she asked.

"That's my father," Alvin said, nodding in the man's direction. "Clinton Cooke."

Goldie looked at Rhys. "Oh, yes."

Rhys nodded. "You'll meet a lot of Weavers and Cookes while you're here. And trust me, some of them you'll never forget. Right, Alvin?"

The boy nodded. "Right you are, Mr. Miller." He trotted off to someone else with a raised hand to give them a drink.

16

Dinner at the main farmhouse was a lively affair, with everyone gathered around a long table in the dining room or the huge table in the kitchen. People also spilled into the parlor, out onto the front porch, and finally onto blankets on the lawn. The food was delicious, and Goldie was grateful for the warm welcome she'd received from the Weavers, Cookes, Cucinottas (Bella's siblings) and the farmhands.

She also met a neighboring family, the Wyndhams, who lived about two miles from the Weaver farm. They had two sons, Taylor and Brandon. The older one, Taylor, kept stealing glances at Phoebe, and vice versa. Goldie smiled putting two and two together.

Goldie sat with Samijo and Arlan on the porch and devoured the food. Between sorting and wading in the creek, she'd worked up an appetite.

Her time at the creek was fun, and no one cared if her dress got wet or she splashed one of them accidentally—or on purpose. There were so many people, it was hard not to get splashed at some point.

She'd watched Rhys, spoke with him amidst the chaos,

then the two retreated back to the main farmhouse. It wasn't long before everyone from the creek had joined them and dinner began.

After dinner, Rhys took her on a tour of the farm. They visited the sorting barn, the milk powder production barn, and the stables. She was impressed by how well everything was organized and how smoothly everything seemed to run.

As they walked back toward the main house, Taylor joined them. "Mr. Miller, might I have a word?"

"Sure." Rhys smiled at her. "Will you excuse me?"

She nodded, and the two men strolled toward the nearest orchard.

While they talked, she looked at the main farmhouse. Another round of sorting was about to begin, but at least it was cooling off. People began to make their way to the barn, including Connie and Hoskins, who spied her and headed her way. "Hello there!" Hoskins called, grinning as they joined her. "Well, what do you think? Did you enjoy your tour?"

"I did. This place is enormous. I can't get over…"

She never got to finish her sentence. A shot rang out and something whizzed past her head.

"Get down!" Rhys, who'd been walking back to them, tackled her to the ground.

Goldie landed with an audible "Oomph!" and was surprised to see Hoskins and Connie on the ground next to them. "What was that?"

Connie looked at her, horrified. "What do you think? A gunshot!"

Rhys looked around as folks came running toward them. "Stay down, all of you." He climbed to his feet and took off toward one of the orchards. He wasn't the only one. Several of the Weaver men were right behind him, one carrying a rifle. She couldn't remember their names and didn't begin to try.

"Goldie, dear," Connie said. "Are you all right?"

She nodded and wondered if it was safe to get to her feet.

"Calvin and one of his sons—Thatcher, was it?—hurried toward them. "Everyone inside until we find out who fired that gun."

Thatcher helped Goldie to her feet as Calvin helped Connie and Hoskins. "Tarnation, Miss Colson," Thatcher said. "That bullet just missed you!"

She looked at the tree behind her. A piece of bark had been shot off one side of it. If she'd been just a few inches to the left, it would have hit her. Her hand flew to her chest at the realization, and she lurched to one side.

"Whoa," Thatcher said. "Steady now."

"Did someone fire a gun?" little Alvin asked as he came running from the barn. "What's happening?"

"Alvin," Calvin barked. "Get on up to Granny Mary's house. Thatcher, take Miss Colson and the rest up too."

"Yes, sir." Thatcher looped an arm around Goldie's, then Connie's, and nodded at Hoskins. "Let's go."

Inside the house, half the people were looking out the windows while the other half were frowning. "When I find out who the fool is that fired that gun…" Granny Mary stopped, scrunched up her face and narrowed her eyes. "Oh, I'm too much of a lady to say it."

Goldie saw the serious expressions of some of the Weavers, then the folks that came from town. Several looked her way and she gulped. "Why would anyone fire a gun?" She was afraid of the answer.

"Now don't you fret, child," Granny Mary said. "Arlan and some of my grandsons have gone after the yahoo that did it. Seems to me everyone's accounted for, but I could be wrong."

"Do you think it's anyone from town, Mary?" Hoskins asked.

"Don't rightly know," she said. "But if it is, he's going to be paying a visit to Sheriff Riley. I won't put up with any shenanigans on my farm. Especially not with this many people here."

Goldie sank into a nearby chair. Why would anyone fire a

gun? Unless, of course, they were aiming to hit something. Was it her?

Connie approached, a glass of lemonade in her hand. "Here, dear, drink this. Land sakes, you're white as a sheet."

Goldie took the glass and drank without question. She was so jittery she couldn't talk.

It wasn't long before Rhys returned to the house and entered the parlor where she and the others sat. "Well?" someone said.

He looked around, then met Goldie's gaze. "What did you find?" she asked.

"Benjamin's son Sebastian is trying to track whomever it was that fired."

Goldie's heart pounded. "So, it was only one person?"

He looked grave. "From what he can tell there were three."

She fought the urge to bury her face in her hands. "I see. What were these three men doing firing at the house and barn?"

His eyebrows knit. "That's what we aim to find out when we catch them. In the meantime, I'm taking you back to town."

"I'm afraid you can't do that, son," Harlan said. "The afternoon train's done come and gone. You'll have to spend the night."

Connie paced. "There's no sense sugarcoating it. We know who fired that gun."

Granny Mary rolled her eyes. "Connie, this is no time for your theatrics. Sit down."

"I can't sit down! I'm too nervous!"

"She's right," Rhys said. "Sit down and try to stay calm. It could have been a misfire."

Goldie stared at him in shock. Did he believe that? Connie was probably right. It was the train robbers, and they took a shot at her. They wanted revenge.

Rhys approached her chair. "I don't want you worrying."

She looked up at him. "How can I not?" She looked around

the crowded room. No one looked happy. This was serious business. So much so she found herself giving Rhys an imploring look that said *do something!* The problem was, she was a much better shot than he was and that might be the reason they sent him back to the farmhouse. "Where are the others?"

"I came back to make sure you were all right. Are you?"

There was no mistaking the concern in his eyes, and her heart melted. She nodded. "The bullet went right past my head. I heard it."

He crouched beside her chair. "Goldie, sweetheart, are you *sure* you're all right?"

She swallowed hard, part of her enjoying the endearment. But she wasn't his sweetheart, she was no one's sweetheart, and at this point might never be. Now more than ever, she had to leave Nowhere. What if someone got hurt on account of her?

"Goldie?" Connie said. "Did you hear what he asked?"

She looked into Rhys' eyes and nodded. "I'm fine. Really."

"All the same," Granny Mary said. "I'm going to make you a cup of tea. I'll have one with you. Maybe it will calm *me* down." The old woman shuffled off, Harlan following.

"I take it random gunfire on this farm isn't a normal thing?" Goldie asked. It was a silly question, she knew, but she was trying to get her mind off someone trying to kill her. What else could it be? She shot one of the train robbers and the rest of his cohorts wanted her dead.

"This is a farm," Rhys said gently. "The only time any shooting happens is if something threatens the livestock or there's target practice."

She nodded and said nothing more.

Within moments, Granny Mary reentered the parlor. Samijo followed carrying a tray laden with cups, saucers and a teapot. She poured Goldie a cup and handed it to her. "Here, drink up."

Goldie took it without question. "When does the next train come through?"

"Tomorrow morning," Samijo said. "Do you want to return to town?"

"Of course she does," Rhys cut in. "And I'll accompany her, then speak to Spencer about what happened."

"When you do, find out if anything's been going on in town," Harlan said.

"There hadn't been before we came here," Rhys took the cup and saucer Samijo offered. "Isn't that right, Hoskins?"

"Yes, we only heard about strangers poking around here."

Harlan scratched the back of his head. "Sebastian spied someone while he was hunting early one morning. Found signs of a campsite. But sometimes hunters come through here, so it's kinda hard to tell on account our property is so big."

Goldie looked from one face to the other. "How big?"

"Thousands of acres, child," Granny Mary said. "Now drink your tea."

Goldie gaped at her. She knew the place was enormous, but she didn't think it was that large. Goldie drank her tea and tried not to fidget. She didn't have enough money to leave Nowhere and wasn't sure where to get some. She could ask Connie and Hoskins for a loan, but when could she pay them back? For all she knew, she didn't have enough money to leave and still have enough left over to spend a few nights in Seattle. What if she went to San Francisco? That was a big city. She could lose herself in it and disappear. If she had the money.

"Goldie?" Rhys said softly. "It's going to be okay."

She looked at him, noticed how tightly she held the handle of her teacup, and set it in its saucer. "Goodness. I guess this is upsetting me more than I thought."

"It's all right. There are plenty of people here. No one's going to hurt you, understand?"

She nodded as reality hit. Everyone was looking at her with sympathy because everyone knew someone was trying to kill her. She wished she had the pink pistol with her, but it didn't occur to her to carry it here. Not with all these people.

She sat back in her chair and stared at the floor. Rhys didn't leave her side. His presence was comforting, but she didn't dare get used to it. He had a home, a family, a life. And she wasn't part of it, never would be. She had to leave.

Still, the realization that she was attracted to him, and the town hit hard. Maybe she could have settled here, worked long enough at the hotel to form a bond with someone, start courting, maybe even get married. But that was impossible now. As soon as she got back to Nowhere, she'd speak to the ticket master at the station and find out how far she could get on what money she had.

"Granny, what about the sorting?"

Goldie looked to see who had spoken. It was Selena.

"We'll wait until Arlan and the others get back, then if it's safe, we'll get back to work." She shuffled to Goldie's chair. "Except you. I think it's best you stay in the house." She glanced at Connie and back. "Just in case Connie's right."

Connie looked at Hoskins and nodded. "I hope I'm not."

"So do I." Goldie glanced at Rhys. His jaw was set, and his eyes had a steely gleam to them. He was angry, anyone could see it. But what could he do? What could any of them do? It was only a matter of time before the train robbers tried again, and everyone in the room with half a brain knew it.

17

Rhys didn't want to let Goldie out of his sight. Unfortunately, she and Connie were right. It had to be the three Coolidge brothers. Who else would take a shot at her? Another half foot, and they would have hit their target. The thought made his blood boil. He bent to her ear. "Is there anything I can get you?"

"Thank you, but no. My stomach is upset now, and not even the tea is helping."

Rhys looked around the room. Everyone had left for the sorting barns except Granny Mary and Harlan. Hoskins even managed to drag Connie out the door—no mean feat, as she was complaining the entire way about her nerves, which quickly turned to her bunions of all things. Either she was afraid to be in the sorting barn or thought she might miss something worth repeating in the parlor. After all, once Arlan and the others returned, they'd come speak with Granny Mary and Harlan first.

Harlan came into the parlor, carrying a slice of pie on a plate. "Are either of you still hungry?"

Goldie shook her head. Rhys gave her a sympathetic look,

then took the plate Harlan offered. "Are you sure?" he asked gently. "It's cherry pie. Looks mighty good."

She shook her head again, so he gave up the attempt.

"Now I don't want you younguns to worry," Harlan said. "Them boys that went after the fool that shot at you are really good at tracking."

Goldie's head came up. "So, you admit they were after me?"

Rhys fought the urge to roll his eyes. "Harlan..."

The old man held up his hand. "I'm afraid Connie Ferguson is right. There ain't no sense sugarcoating something like this. After all my years as a lawman, it's best to face facts."

Goldie got to her feet and approached him. "You were a lawman?"

"Sure was. Most of my time was spent in Clear Creek. I was the sheriff there."

She turned to Rhys with an odd smile. "Is this why you know so much about that town?"

He shrugged. "Well, Harlan did live there a long time."

Harlan laughed. "Make no mistake. Clear Creek has its quirks. Not to mention some interesting residents. But the people there are kind, welcoming and will do anything for you. I have nothing bad to say about the town. So what if people think it's strange?"

She smiled again, but it looked forced. He couldn't blame her. She must be terrified, poor thing.

Rhys motioned to the sofa against one wall. "Is there anything you want, anything you need?" He hoped he wasn't being repetitive, but he was nervous as a cat and itched to do something, *anything*, to resolve this. But he was no tracker and, unfortunately, not that great of a shot. He wished he was.

He smiled at Goldie. "At least you didn't have a gun at the time. The shooter would probably be dead."

She stared at him a moment, half-smiling. "Is that supposed to make me feel better?"

He stuck his hands in his pockets and began to pace. "To be truthful, I think it's supposed to make *me* feel better. If you'd had a gun, you would probably use it."

"Not necessarily." She returned to her chair. "I'm good with a rifle and fair with a pistol, but I wouldn't want to shoot anyone. Not unless I had to."

"This may have been one of those times. Do you own a weapon?" Harlan asked.

"I have a pistol. That is, Ben Ferguson had one. I practiced with it last week."

"Good, I'd keep practicing. But I'd see if Spencer or his brother Clayton can go with you. Or Rhys here." Harlan nodded at him.

Rhys didn't want to mention his poor shooting. Instead, he nodded and took his hands out of his pockets. He was still pacing, though. Maybe he should eat the pie Harlan gave him.

Goldie left her chair again and went to a window.

"I wouldn't do that if I were you," Harlan advised. "If one of them varmints is still out there, the last place you want to be is near a window. You don't want them to be able to see you."

Rhys gently took her arm and led her to the other side of the room. "Sit here," he instructed. "It's safer."

She wrung her hands and sat. "I can't live like this," she blurted. "I don't want to go day in and day out wondering if someone's going to take a shot at me. What if it happens again?"

"Now, now," Harlan soothed. "Don't get upset. You wouldn't be the first woman that needed some protection."

"And I'm happy to do it," Rhys said. "I already volunteered."

She stared at him a moment, left the chair and paced.

"Don't go near the window," Harlan warned.

She stopped and turned to them. "This is ridiculous. I've got to do something." She glanced at the nearest window, then growled.

"We know you're upset, Goldie," Rhys said. "But that's not going to help the situation. All we can do is wait for Arlan and the others to return and see what they have to say. Either they came up empty-handed, or they know where the outlaws are heading. There's also the possibility it wasn't them. Some of the cowhands have rifles and pistols with them when they're watching the cattle."

She slumped onto the sofa. "I suppose you're right. But I do hate waiting."

"How about another cup of tea?" Harlan offered.

She nodded without a word and rubbed her temple with the ball of her thumb.

Rhys watched her a moment, then joined her on the sofa. "I'm sorry I didn't say anything to you before."

She stopped massaging. "About?"

"The outlaws." He sighed. "I volunteered to protect you. Spencer deputized me so I could do it properly."

She gave him a blank stare. "You did?" She folded her hands and rested them in her lap. "When did you do this?"

"After you arrived in town." He sat back and tried not to fidget. He wasn't sure who was more nervous, him or her. "What happened to you didn't set well with me. I don't know why—it could've happened to anyone. But the thought of you being in harm's way…" He stood and faced her. "You've suffered enough, Goldie. I don't want to see you suffer anymore."

Her face softened as she looked at him. "Thank you. That's… one of the nicest things anyone has said to me. Considering we barely know each other."

His eyes flicked to the dining room and back. "Would you like to get to know me?"

Her hand flew to her chest, as if he just made the most absurd suggestion. "Oh, Mr. Miller…"

"Rhys."

She blushed head to toe. "Rhys. I'm not staying. How can I?"

He thought a moment. "I believe I understand. There's no place to hide in Nowhere."

She blushed again. "That's part of it."

Did she think he couldn't protect her? That no one could? "Our town has seen its share of trouble, Goldie. We're not a bunch of greenhorns that don't know what to do about it."

"I didn't say you were. Please don't take offense."

He sat in a nearby chair. She was trying to be brave, but he could see the fear in her eyes, no matter how well she tried to cover it up. "We'll do what we can."

"Like what? Stay at the hotel with me? It's not only improper but…"

"Practical." He left the chair, went to the side of one window and peeked out. "If I stayed at the hotel with you, at least you'd have some protection."

"I have a pistol," she stated, chin held high.

"And you're mighty good with it. Still, you're a little thing and could be overpowered easily."

Her jaw dropped. "Are you suggesting one of those train robbers is going to crawl through the window to shoot me?" Her voice cracked on the last word.

"That's exactly what they might try. Which is why you shouldn't be alone."

"What?"

He thought a moment and rubbed his chin. "Yes, if you're surrounded by people, they wouldn't dare try to…"

She pointed at the window. "And what do you think they just did? They shot at me, Rhys, despite all the people!"

Okay, she had a point. "That doesn't mean we can't do anything about it, sweetheart."

She lowered her hand and sank onto the sofa. "Like what?"

"There are plenty of people here on this farm, all of which

know they shot at you. How likely are they to try again? You could always stay here, and I'll stay with you."

Her jaw dropped again. "What?"

"Unless you'd rather go back to town and be with Connie and Hoskins."

Her eyes rounded to saucers. He was trying to make a point, and she was finally getting it. "Oh. I think I'm the only one there other than those two. I know there's one other woman from the train that's still in Nowhere. Connie said she came to visit relatives. I've hardly seen her. I think Dinwiddie is her name."

"Sometimes we get a lot of folks staying in the hotel," Rhys said. "Now's not one of those times."

Goldie blinked, as if taking in everything he'd said so far. In his mind, the Weaver farm was the safest place. Nowhere had twice as many people, but everybody was going about their business, and no one would want to worry about being shot by a stray bullet. What if the train robbers sent one of their lot to town, while the other two patrolled here looking for her? It wasn't as if Goldie could hide in a local business all day if she were in town. At least here everyone would be on the lookout for suspicious activity. "I'll talk to Granny Mary and Harlan and see what they say."

She stared at him, her mouth slowly dropping open.

"What is it?"

She shook her head. "I don't know what I did wrong. It was an accident; don't they know that?"

He sat on the sofa next to her and took her hands in his. "How could they?"

She shook her head again. "I don't know. The other two were already leaving the car. And that's when the third shot Ben Ferguson. He took aim at me as I was grabbing Ben's gun, and it went off."

"It was an accident, honey. They don't know it was, and I'm afraid no amount of explaining will deter them."

Her eyes misted with tears. "Thank you, Rhys. Thank you for trying to protect me."

He reached up, brushed a wisp of hair from her face and smiled. "It's my pleasure."

Goldie smiled back, and though it was weak, he could see the determination in her eyes growing. She would fight with everything she had, was his guess. She might be a tiny thing, but she was a spitfire. Good.

"You stay here, honey. I'm going to go speak with Harlan and Granny Mary."

"I'm going with you." She got to her feet and headed for the dining room. "Coming?"

He chuckled to himself and followed.

In the kitchen Harlan was just filling a teacup. "Here you are. Sorry this was taking so long but I had to help Ebba with something."

"Where is she?" Rhys asked.

"She went down to the sorting barn to tell what folks she could find to stay inside someplace. She also wanted to know where Goldie might feel more comfortable, here at the main house or at Calvin and Bella's."

Goldie glanced between the two. "My things are at Bella's. I don't mind staying there."

"Harlan, I'd like to stay there too," Rhys said. "I know they have plenty of rooms with most of the children married and gone now.

Harlan laughed. "Not all of them went far, remember? They're still on the farm, just in their own homes."

He smiled and nodded. "True, which is one more reason I want to stay at Calvin's. The more men in the house, the better."

"Well, suit yourself." Harlan scratched his head. "I'm sure Calvin or one of the boys has an extra gun you can have. I thought I heard Spencer issued you one. Are you a deputy now?"

Rhys reached into his pocket, pulled out the deputy's star and showed it to him.

Harlan took it from him and pinned it on Rhys' vest. "There. Now you're official. Maybe them train robbers will think twice if they see that."

He looked at the star, then at Goldie. "Does it make you feel any better?"

She looked sheepish. "What would is if I had a rifle."

Harlan's bushy eyebrows went up. "You're better with one of those than a pistol?"

"She sure is," Rhys admitted. "In fact, she's a far better shot than Hoskins or me."

Goldie smiled. "My father was a Texas Ranger."

"Was he now?" Harlan said in delight. "And he taught you how to shoot?"

"He did. And it's a good thing. It's something that can come in mighty handy."

"I'm afraid this is one of those times." Harlan looked at Rhys. "I suppose I can muster up a gun for you. After all, there's no sense wearing that star if you haven't got a firearm at your side, now is there?"

Rhys closed his eyes as heat crept up his neck and into his cheeks. "I suppose not."

18

Goldie caught Rhys' embarrassment and her heart went out to him. Harlan excused himself and went upstairs to fetch a gun, giving Rhys a moment to check the window again. She knew he was trying to compose himself and she hoped he wasn't too put out.

"I think I see Arlan and his twin sons coming back," he announced.

She joined him at the window, but he put an arm out to stop her. When he looked at her, he shook his head and gently pushed her to the side, away from the window. "Oh, yes—sorry."

"We can't be too careful until we find out what he has to say." He headed for the front door. "Stay here." He disappeared into the front hall, leaving her standing with her heart in her throat.

She didn't like people fussing over her, and especially didn't like feeling helpless. If there were men out there wanting to kill her, what could she do about it? Yes, she was a good shot, but as Rhys and Harlan pointed out, she could be overpowered and then what? She wasn't bulletproof.

Goldie went to the side of the window and peeked out the

curtains. Arlan and two other men were speaking with Rhys. She thought of the endearments he'd used earlier and smiled. She'd never had a man talk to her that way, and it sent tingles up her spine and made her belly warm. He was handsome, so that was part of it. But he was trying to calm her, make her feel better. Words like "sweetheart" and "honey" were used in a general sense, not in affection.

She sighed and returned to the sofa. She wanted to leave the house, join the men and find out what they discovered. But Rhys would get upset and so would Arlan.

"Here we are." Harlan re-entered the parlor and looked around. "Where's Rhys?"

"Outside with Arlan and his sons."

"Good." He set the pistol on a low table in front of the sofa. "I'll be right back."

She sighed as he too left the room. "Well, this is just peachy." She crossed her arms.

"Don't be troubled, child," Granny Mary said as she entered and sat on the sofa. "Harlan's gun." She picked it up. "What's it doing here?"

"He was going to let Rhys use it tonight."

"For what?"

"To…" Goldie sighed again. "… protect me."

The old woman slowly nodded. "I see. Well, that was right nice of him to loan it. Harlan loves this gun. It's seen a lot of action in its time."

She smiled. "When he was a sheriff?"

"Yes, and then some. You don't live on a farm this big and not have trouble now and then. This is no different." Granny Mary smiled at her. "How are you holding up?"

"I'm fine," she lied. In truth, she wished she had the pink pistol with her. For a thing that was supposed to bring love, it could sure come in handy about now. She didn't believe love came with it but thank goodness a box of Smith & Wesson .32

smokeless cartridges did. Unfortunately, she left the pistol and bullets in her room at Bella's.

"Don't fret, child," Granny Mary said, interrupting her thoughts. "Arlan will let everyone know what's going on."

"Will they fetch the sheriff?"

"Goodness, no, but they can telegraph him. We'll have to wait until tomorrow when the train comes through in the morning. If you'd like to be on it, we can arrange that. With a heavy guard, if need be."

She sat and hung her head. "The Coolidge brothers are going to drive me around the bend."

Granny Mary put an arm around her. "I haven't heard of them. Did Spencer tell you they were dangerous?"

She shook her head, trying to remember everything the sheriff said. Part of her still didn't think that Herbert, Dale, and their cousin Dilbert could be all that dangerous. But Jonny Coolidge proved he was by shooting Theodore and his father Ben. Too bad Ben hadn't been wearing the pink pistol. But he was going to find the owner and return it, so it wasn't his to wear.

"What's the matter, child?"

Goldie put a hand to one hot cheek. If she were a man, would she be carrying around a pink-handled revolver? Probably not. "It's nothing." The front door opened, and she sprang to her feet, careful to avoid the window as she headed for the front hall. "Did you find anything?"

Arlan took off his hat, wiped his brow with his sleeve and looked her in the eyes. "We found the remains of another campsite."

Rhys stepped forward. "Sebastian, Arlan's nephew, can track, and said there are definitely three men. Looks like they've been on the farm for the last few days, at least according to the campsites we found."

"They keep moving around," Arlan said. "Maybe they're hopin' to retrieve their brother's body to bury him themselves, considerin' the train stopped here. But Jonny Coolidge is in Nowhere. I suspect he was buried at least a week ago."

"One would think they'd go to Nowhere to find out," Goldie said.

Arlan shook his head. "No one said this gang had brains."

"They don't sound like it."

"But that's what could make them so dangerous," Rhys said. "They just start shooting with no thought. There's no reasoning with someone like that." He closed the distance between them. "Which is one more reason they're hanging around. One of them must have recognized you and took the opportunity to settle the score."

"That's if these are the same men," Arlan put in. "They might not be."

Goldie took a deep breath. She hated not knowing what was going on. "What do we do?"

"I'm going to escort you to Calvin and Bella's place," Rhys said. "We'll stay there. So will a few other family members."

"They'll have to get through a passel of Weavers if'n they want to get to ya," Arlan said. "We could be wrong in all this, and they're just poachers tryin' to avoid detection. We've had some on the place before. But if it is the Coolidge gang, better to be safe than sorry."

Goldie nodded. She couldn't agree more. "When will we go to Calvin and Bella's house?"

"As soon as it gets dark," Rhys said.

"But won't that make it harder to see them?"

"And harder to see you," he pointed out.

She nodded. "Oh, right." Her heart sank. The thought that the train robbers might still be lurking about seemed so far away at first. Probably because they were seen out here and not in town. But now she was here, and suddenly the threat was real. What would she do if they tried something? She couldn't risk anyone getting hurt. There were women and children in the sorting barn at this very moment. What if Herbert,

Dale, and Dilbert got it into their fool heads to hold one of the Weaver women or children hostage just to get to her? How revenge-driven were they?

That is, if indeed the men sneaking around the farm were the Coolidges.

"Harlan," Granny Mary said. "Your gun?" She held it up.

"Oh, yes." He took it and approached Rhys. "Here, you'll need this. Be careful, it's loaded."

Rhys took the gun. "Got a gun belt?"

"Sure do—I'll go fetch it." Harlan disappeared up the staircase.

"I'd best get to the sortin' barn," Arlan said. "Calvin and Bella will take precautions to make sure their house is safe." He put his hand on Goldie's shoulder. "You'll be fine."

She took another shaky breath. Easy for him to say—he wasn't the one getting shot at. "Thank you."

He nodded and headed out the door. Granny Mary closed it behind him, then turned to Goldie. "Now don't fret. The sorting will be done in about an hour, and after it grows dark Rhys and one of my sons or grandsons will escort you to Calvin's."

Goldie pinched the bridge of her nose. "I feel awful about this."

Granny Mary took her by the arm. "Don't. Folks out here look after each other. Doesn't matter if the bad is happening to you, one of us, or Connie or Hoskins. We're in this together. Everyone that lives on this farm, around it, and in Nowhere."

Goldie smiled. "That's a lot of people, isn't it?"

"Not when you compare it to Kansas City."

She smiled. "No, I suppose not." Goldie turned to Rhys. "Thank you again." Her voice was almost a whisper, and she hoped she didn't do something silly tonight like cry.

Harlan ushered them back into the parlor where they would wait it out until nightfall. She sat on the sofa next to Rhys, and she wondered if his parents would head back to

Nowhere tomorrow with them. And here she was, the source of trouble and angst at a time that was celebrated around here. She still thought she'd be better off taking the first train west and getting as far away from Nowhere as possible.

When it came time for Rhys to take her to Calvin's, they were joined by Daniel, Granny Mary's youngest, and his son Ulysses. They left the house, the night deep and dark with stars shining like diamonds in the sky. She felt safe in their company. Their steps were slow and measured, their boots thudding across the yard, then crunching on the dirt and gravel trail that led to Calvin's place. The lanterns they carried illuminated the path in front of them, casting long shadows on the ground.

Goldie shivered and hugged herself, feeling cold seep into her bones even though it was a warm night. Rhys noticed her discomfort and took off his coat, draping it over her shoulders. She blushed and smiled gratefully. The coat was warm and smelled of him, and she felt a strange flutter in her stomach as she breathed in his scent. *Oh, no, this isn't good. I can't afford to be attracted to someone now! Besides, I'm leaving!*

They arrived at Calvin's house and as soon as they approached the front door, Calvin opened it and stood before them, a smile on his face. "Made it, I see. Good." He stepped aside to let them in. As soon as they were, his sons Alastair and Thatcher slipped into the night, each carrying a rifle.

"Where are they going?" she asked.

"To make sure there ain't no one sneaking around that ought not to be." Calvin closed the door.

Goldie nodded and looked around the cozy house, feeling the warmth of the cookstove that still had a fire in it.

Bella came down the hall from the kitchen with a smile and a nod, and they settled in the parlor. "I've made some tea," she said. "I'll get it."

Goldie watched her go and sighed in relief. So far, so good.

When Bella returned and served everyone, Goldie sipped

her tea, letting the warmth spread through her body. She looked around the parlor, taking in her surroundings. It was strange to think that just a few weeks ago; she had never set foot in Nowhere, had met none of these people.

Rhys caught her eye, gave her a reassuring smile, and she got a flutter in her belly. Oh, for crying out loud, not again. She reached for a cookie. Bella brought a large plateful not long ago, and half of them had been eaten already.

No one said much. They didn't have to. Each was as apprehensive as she was, sans the tingles up the spine every time Rhys looked their way. But when he glanced at her, it was all she could do not to melt a little despite the circumstances. He was being protective, but she sensed it might be more than that. Then again, it wouldn't be the first time she was wrong about something, and probably was. *Don't be a fool, Goldie. You can't stay. Think of all the people you're putting in danger.*

She looked around the parlor, her heart in her throat. She had no choice but to leave Nowhere and the Weavers behind.

19

Rhys watched Goldie carefully. She was putting up a good front, but he could tell she was frightened. Who wouldn't be? But as Arlan and some of the other Weaver men tracked the strangers to different parts of the farm, the poachers (if they were poachers) would have hightailed it out of there. If it was the Coolidge brothers and their cousin Dilbert, perhaps not. They might be out for blood, and if that was the case, Goldie was in danger.

"I'll take the first watch," Calvin announced. "Rhys, ya can stay in the room across the hall from Goldie."

He nodded. "I can take the second watch."

"No, ya have yer post," Calvin said. "One of the boys will keep an eye out."

His eyes darted to the door. "Is anyone else coming to help?"

"Arlan's boys Justin and Jason."

"But that will leave their families unprotected," Rhys said.

"They'll be fine." Calvin smiled at Goldie. "Ya holdin' up?"

She opened her mouth to speak but nothing came out at first. "W-well. It seems everyone is making a big fuss."

"Of course, we are," Bella said. "Someone shot at you!"

"What if they were shooting at something else?"

"The only other ones there were Connie, Hoskins and myself," Rhys said. "That bullet hit the tree behind you. It was close, Goldie. Too close."

She shuddered and sat back.

He didn't care how it looked; he gave her leg a pat. "But you don't have to worry. We'll take care of this."

"And what about when we get back to town?" she asked.

"I'll see you're kept safe." Rhys leaned toward her. "I promise." He realized his hand was still on her leg and quickly removed it. He noted Calvin watched with interest but said nothing. "Well, what say we turn in?" he said to break the sudden silence. "Goldie, there's no sense worrying yourself. Go upstairs and try to get some sleep."

She rose from the sofa. "I'll try, but I'm not promising I will."

He escorted her from the parlor to the staircase as Calvin and Bella spoke quietly. "Everything will be fine. These people know what they're doing and so do I."

She looked at Harlan's gun belt. "I hope you don't have to use that."

He put his hand on the holster. "So do I."

She smiled stiffly. "Because you're a bad shot?"

"No, because I'm afraid you'll come running out of your room and show me up. Who knows, you might have to rescue *me*." He hoped she didn't take his remark wrong.

He was rewarded with a bigger smile. "Let's hope not. I'm liable to shoot whatever moves."

He shook his head and looked into her eyes. "You're too good a shot and besides, you're a thinker. I can't imagine you reacting and shooting willy-nilly."

"What if they do?"

Unable to help himself, he put his hand on her shoulder. "I wouldn't worry. You're bulletproof."

"I'm nothing of the kind. I'm lucky I didn't get shot right after Theodore's father did."

He started up the stairs, motioning her to follow. "What I'm trying to say is, you're stronger than you think."

They reached the top of the stairs, and she sighed. "I'm glad you think so." She proceeded down the hall to her room.

He went to the room opposite, peeked inside, then spied a chair at the end of the hall and went to fetch it. As he took his post outside Goldie's room, he thought about her safety. What if the robbers went after the train again? Any outlaw with half a brain wouldn't. But the Coolidges weren't known for their smarts. Goldie knew it too. He'd seen the fear in her eyes earlier and it had made his heart race. She'd already suffered a great deal, and didn't need any more. Maybe that's why he'd been so protective of her after he found out what happened to her.

He thought about his promise earlier to keep her safe, no matter what. But as he scanned his surroundings, he couldn't shake the feeling that something was off. Maybe the train robbers were still sneaking around. Would Thatcher and Alastair run into them while they patrolled the area?

He tried to distract himself by listening to the night sounds coming through the open window at the end of the hall. Crickets chirped and the occasional owl hooted. But his mind kept drifting back to Goldie, to how her blonde hair fell around her face like a halo, to the curve of her waist beneath her dress. He cursed himself silently. What was wrong with him? He couldn't afford to be distracted like this, not when her life was in danger. But the more he tried to push the thoughts away, the more they persisted.

Unable to take it anymore, he got up and walked across the hall to her room. He knocked softly on the door, waiting for her to answer.

"Rhys?" Her voice was soft, almost hesitant on the other side of the door.

He opened it and stepped inside her room. She was sitting up in bed; the covers pulled to her chest. She looked so vulnerable, so delicate, and his heart ached at the thought of anyone hurting her. "Sorry, but there's something I need to check." He crossed the room to the open window and closed it. "Some of the rooms are accessible from the outside for a good climber. Best keep this one closed."

She stared at him wide-eyed. "Yes, of course." She pulled the covers up a little higher. "Good night."

Rhys hesitated, feeling like there was something more he needed to do before leaving her alone. He leaned against the windowsill, looking at her in the soft moonlight that shone through her window. "Goldie, I'm sorry if I'm making you uncomfortable. That's not my intention. It's just that I can't help worrying about you."

She shook her head and smiled. "You're not making me uncomfortable. On the contrary, I feel safe when you're around."

Rhys felt a weight lift off his shoulders at her words. "Good. I want you to feel safe and protected."

She lowered her gaze, her fingers playing with the edge of the blanket. "Can I ask you something?"

"Of course."

She looked up at him, her brown eyes searching his face. "Do you ever think about… living someplace else?"

He shrugged. "This is my home. My family is here."

She nodded. "Of course. It was a silly question."

"Why do you ask?" He took a step toward the bed. He should say goodnight again and leave. But he'd felt his heart skip at her words. He'd thought about her, more than he should have, and some of those thoughts were of the two of them in a little house somewhere, starting a life together. He tried to keep his feelings in check all day, knowing that it was inappropriate to have such thoughts about a woman he was supposed to be protecting.

But in that moment, he couldn't hold back any longer. He approached the bed. "You'll be all right. No one, and I mean no one, is going to harm you."

She nodded, her eyes locked with his. "Good night."

"Good night," he whispered. But before he could turn to leave, he felt her small hand wrap around his wrist. He looked down at her, surprised at the sudden contact. "Is there something else?" he asked, trying to keep his voice even.

She hesitated, gnawing on her bottom lip. "I know this might sound silly, but… would you mind staying here just for a little while? I don't think I can sleep."

Rhys felt his heart race at the request. He knew it was a bad idea, knew he should go back to his post, but he couldn't resist the urge to comfort her. He moved to the side of the bed and sat down, trying to keep a safe distance between them. "Is there anything you'd like to talk about?" he asked, trying to sound casual.

She shook her head, looking down at her hands. "I… I feel like I'm constantly on edge. Like I'm waiting for something bad to happen."

Rhys nodded, understanding all too well. "It's normal to feel that way, given what's happened. But I promise you, we're doing everything we can to keep you safe."

"I know," she whispered, still not meeting his gaze. "It's just… I feel so alone sometimes. Like there's no one I can talk to. And then I just feel, well, stupid."

Rhys felt a pang of guilt at that. He'd been so focused on protecting her, he hadn't stopped to consider her emotional needs. "You can talk to me," he breathed, reaching out to move a strand of hair out of her eyes. His fingers brushed against her skin, sending shivers down his spine. *Uh-oh. Time to leave!*

She closed her eyes at his touch. "Rhys," she whispered.

Too late. Without thinking, he leaned in and pressed his lips to hers. It was a gentle kiss, but it left him feeling like he was on fire. He pulled back, looking into her eyes. "I'm sorry," he said, his voice thick. "I shouldn't have done that."

"No," she breathed. "Don't be sorry." She put a hand to her mouth and swallowed hard. "I should have told you to leave."

Rhys felt his resolve crumbling as he cupped her face with his hand. "You're safe." Then he stood and marched out of the room as fast as he could.

As soon as he closed the door behind him, Bella appeared at the top of the stairs, making him jump. "Rhys, what's the matter?" She looked at Goldie's door. "Is she okay?"

Rhys hoped he wasn't crimson. "Yes. I just made sure the window was closed and locked." *And I should make sure I don't set food in Goldie's room the rest of the night!*

Bella looked him over. "You plan to stay up all night?"

He leaned against the wall. "Most of it."

"No, you can't. You will not be able to look after her tomorrow. Rest for a few hours while Calvin and the boys take a watch. Then you can stand watch with Justin and Jason."

He forgot about Arlan's sons coming to help. "Fine. I'll do that. But I'm keeping my door open."

She smiled. "You like her, don't you?"

His eyebrows shot up in alarm. He'd forgotten how perceptive Bella Weaver was. "I beg your pardon?"

She smiled slyly and nodded. "You know, she *is* a mail-order bride without a husband. Maybe you should think about that." With a parting smile, she went down the hall to her room.

Rhys couldn't believe what he was hearing. Bella was suggesting he consider Goldie as a potential wife? He shook his head ruefully. It was ridiculous. For one thing, he was her protector, and she'd suffered enough since coming here, including his kiss.

Okay, that was a big mistake. The last thing she needed was to be courted by someone like him. Besides, until recently, marriage was a commitment he wasn't sure he was ready for.

But as he walked across the hall to his room, he couldn't shake the feeling that Bella might be onto something. Goldie was different from any other woman he'd met. She was strong, resilient, and kind-hearted. And he couldn't deny the intense attraction he felt for her.

Rhys lay in bed, his thoughts racing, unable to sleep. He had a strong desire to see her again, to be close to her. He knew it was a bad idea, but couldn't help himself.

He got up and paused at the threshold of his door, listening for any signs of movement from either in the house or outside. All he could hear was Goldie's soft breathing coming from her room, and he noticed her door was slightly ajar. From the sounds of it, she was sleeping peacefully. He felt a pang of guilt standing there listening, but he couldn't resist the urge to be closer to her.

Rhys wanted to kick himself. He was being foolish, giving in to his attraction, that's all. Besides, he'd already kissed her. What did she think of him now? He rolled his eyes, not wanting to know the answer, and went back to bed. Once he crawled in he tried to relax. He had to get at least some sleep before taking his watch with Arlan's sons. His kiss didn't matter, nor how he felt about Goldie. All that did was keeping her safe. He just hoped he could keep his heart safe in the process.

20

Goldie made it through the night without incident. She went downstairs to breakfast, making sure not to make eye contact with Rhys. His kiss had startled her at first, but she had to admit she liked it. Maybe a little too much.

Her cheeks heated as she made her way around the kitchen table where Calvin and Bella's family were seating themselves. The morning was already warm, and she wondered how hot it would be today. She also wondered how she was going to avoid Rhys. How could she look him in the eye after last night? He kissed her—and she let him! Well, considering the circumstances, maybe he thought he was comforting her. But a hug would have sufficed.

She sat and realized both were improper. He was in her room; she was in bed, enough said. What if someone had discovered them? What if…

"Did you sleep well?" Bella asked. Her eyes flicked to Rhys and back as she smiled at Goldie.

She gulped. "Um, yes. Thank you for asking." She glanced at Rhys, caught his rueful smile, then looked at the blue and white checkered tablecloth. So, was he sorry he'd kissed her?

"Coffee?" Bella held up the pot.

Goldie shoved a cup and saucer toward her and watched Bella fill the cup. "Thank you."

"Cream and sugar are on the table." Bella returned the pot to the stove, eyeing Rhys as she did.

Goldie wasn't sure what that was about and didn't care. She wanted to forget about last night and concentrate on what today might bring.

As she sipped her coffee, she sensed the weight of Rhys' gaze on her. She stole a glance at him and caught him staring at her, his brow furrowed as though he was trying to read her thoughts.

She quickly averted her gaze and focused on the breakfast that was being served. Pancakes, scrambled eggs, and bacon filled the table, and the aroma made her stomach growl with hunger. She put a hand to her belly, noticed Bella's amused smile, then froze when Rhys sat in the chair next to her. She smiled at him in greeting but nothing more. Now what was she going to do? She wouldn't be surprised if she blushed throughout the meal!

As soon as Calvin said the blessing and platters of food made their way around the table, she piled her plate with food, trying to ignore Rhys' presence beside her.

"Can we talk?" he whispered, his breath tickling her ear.

Goldie gulped and nodded, her heart thumping. "After breakfast."

"Fine."

"Are we returning to Nowhere this morning?"

"I'll speak to Harlan and some of the other men, then we'll see."

Unable to help it, she looked at him. "Do you think it's safer if we stay here?"

He hesitated, as if he wasn't sure how to word what he had to say next. "We… would have a better chance of catching them if we do."

She blanched. Did they want to use her as bait? "Why?"

"There are more people here to look out for you. Besides, it's not as if the Coolidges are stupid enough to try anything more here, but that doesn't mean they aren't still around. If I were them, I'd be waiting for the moment you leave, then try to get you once you got back to town."

She felt her face go pale. "I see."

"Let's talk about this later." Rhys looked at her food. "Eat up."

She stared at her pancakes and didn't know which was more frightening, being used as bait to catch the Coolidge gang, or the memory of Rhys' kiss. Though the latter was more pleasurable than the former.

She stole glances at him out of the corner of her eye. What else did he want to talk about? Unless it was about the kiss.

As soon as breakfast was done, Rhys excused them both and led her to the front porch. "What happened last night was my fault," he said, his eyes boring into hers. "I apologize. I acted less than a gentleman."

She looked down, unable to meet his gaze. "I... don't know. I was upset, and you were there. I guess I got carried away."

"Carried away?" His voice was low and husky, and she felt a shiver run down her spine.

"I could have stopped you," she whispered, her heart racing.

He took a step closer, and Goldie could feel the heat emanating from his body. "It won't happen again. I just wanted to apologize. The fault is mine." He swallowed hard, his eyes resting on her lips. Good grief, he looked ready to kiss her again! And doggone it, she wanted him to. But no, she couldn't let him, and didn't dare get too close to him. It would just be her luck those Coolidge brothers would be watching and decide to shoot Rhys instead. An eye-for-an-eye sort of thing.

"Fine, apology accepted." Goldie whispered.

Rhys nodded, taking a step back. "Good. Now, about staying here… I think it's for the best."

She nodded in agreement. "I don't want to be caught off guard again. And if it means catching the Coolidge gang, then so much the better."

He smiled. "That's the spirit. I'll talk to Harlan and see what our next move should be."

She watched as Rhys walked away, his broad shoulders disappearing into the house. She briefly pondered if they would ever have a chance at something more than just a kiss. For all she knew, it was just one of those things, and he would forget about it soon enough. Would she? She didn't know and knew she shouldn't think about it. Right now, they had a job to do and a danger to avoid. She would have to push other thoughts aside and focus on the task at hand.

Goldie took a deep breath and turned to go back into the house, ready to face whatever came their way.

ONCE AGAIN, Rhys wanted to kick himself. Had he confused her? Would she want anything to do with him after all this was over and they hopefully had the Coolidges behind bars? If Bella hadn't made her comment last night about Goldie being a mail-order bride without a husband, he might have gotten some proper sleep. But what snatches he managed weren't enough, and he was feeling a little rummy. He could ill afford to go through the day with his senses dulled.

They might have already seen the last of the Coolidge brothers, but there were no guarantees. He needed to make sure Goldie was safe, and he would do whatever it took to keep her that way. Even if it meant sacrificing any chance of a future with her.

He grimaced. Not that he'd had one to begin with. Not after last night.

He left Calvin and Bella's and found Harlan and the other men gathered in the main farmhouse's barn, discussing what to do next. Rhys filled them in on what he and Goldie had discussed, and they all agreed it was best if she stayed put for a while. "Good call," Harlan said, nodding in agreement. "We can post a few lookouts and watch for any suspicious activity. I'd rather not get folks upset, so we'll keep this quiet and let everyone know to just be careful. After yesterday, the fools should be long gone. It's obvious we know they're out there."

"Yeah," Arlan agreed. "But there's foolish, then just plain stupid, and we still ain't sure what we're dealin' with."

Rhys sighed. "That said, we also have a better chance of catching them if Goldie stays here. If they are indeed that dumb, they'll try again. And between all of us, it should be easy enough to apprehend them."

"Good point." Harlan turned to Arlan and his twin sons Justin and Jason. "What do you think?"

"I think they're long gone and like you, we don't want folks getting all upset for nothing," Justin commented. "Tarnation, Granny Mary's liable to sit on the front porch all day with a shotgun."

Rhys smiled as he pictured the old woman ready to do battle. Granny Mary could be mighty feisty when she wanted to. "So, we'll be quiet about this. Can Goldie sort this afternoon?"

Harlan shrugged. "I don't see why not, if a few of the boys patrol the area around the sorting barn. So long as there's a lot of people around, she should be safe enough. She was near one of the orchards last night and with only a couple of people when that shot was fired."

Everyone nodded their agreement. "All right, then." Arlan turned to his sons. "You boys get some of yer cousins and position yerselves so yer in each other's sight and can keep an eye on things. The last thing I want is for everyone 'round here to get all fidgety and trigger happy."

"Will do, Pa." Justin slapped his brother on the shoulder, and they were off.

Rhys sighed in relief. "Thank you, gentlemen, I appreciate it. I'll speak with my father about my staying behind when they return to town."

"You could always go with them," Harlan suggested.

He shook his head. "I made Goldie a promise, and I aim to see it through. I'll keep her safe until she decides what she wants to do."

"What do you mean?" Arlan asked.

Rhys tried not to fidget. "Whether she stays in Nowhere. I know Ben Ferguson was heading to Seattle. I'm not sure what Goldie's plans are, but I know she's leaning toward going someplace where she'd have a better chance of finding work and supporting herself." He shrugged. "Let's face it, there's no work for her here unless Connie and Hoskins want to keep her on, and we all know how fickle Connie can be."

The men nodded. "Hoskins ain't much better," Harlan said. "Okay, fine, stay on if'n you like, but I have a feeling those train robbers have moved on."

Arlan shook his head. "We've been wrong before, Harlan."

The old man shrugged. "True. Let's hope I'm not."

Rhys thanked them and went back to the house, his mind still on Goldie. He needed to talk to her, to make sure she understood the gravity of the situation.

He found her in the kitchen washing dishes. There was no sign of Bella. "Hello," he said as he closed the back door. "Are you doing all right?"

She looked up at him and forced a smile. "Yes, I'm fine. Just trying to keep busy. Bella had to run to the main farmhouse for a moment."

He looked around. "You mean you're alone?"

"No, Thatcher's wife Mia is upstairs and so is Selena. Phoebe went with Bella."

Rhys nodded. "That's good. I just spoke with Harlan and some of the others. They agree that it's best if you stay here a while longer."

Goldie's face fell. "Oh, I see. I guess I was secretly hoping I could return to town with you and the others."

"I know, and I'm sorry. But we don't know if those train robbers are still around, and if they are, they might come after you again. Hopefully we'll know more at the end of the day."

Goldie sighed. "I understand. I just feel so useless here."

Rhys stepped closer. "You're not useless, Goldie. You're helping Bella out, and you're safe. That's what matters right now."

She looked up at him, her eyes softening. "Thank you, Rhys. You're always so kind to me."

His heart raced as she looked up at him with those big brown eyes. The vulnerability in them made him want to take her in his arms and never let go. But he knew he couldn't, not when danger might still lurk around them. He cleared his throat. "I need to talk to you about something else. It's important."

Goldie looked up at him, her expression serious. "What is it?"

"I need to know what your plans are. After all this is over, I mean."

She frowned. "I don't understand."

"Are you planning on leaving Nowhere? Going to Seattle, like Ben Ferguson wanted?"

Goldie bit her lip. "I… I haven't decided. I just want to get through this first."

"But do you like Nowhere?"

She blinked a few times. "I suppose."

Rhys knew he should shut up now—wait until this was over, as she was doing, then seek the right opportunity to see what her plans were. His heart might get ahead of his mind, and he didn't want to do or say anything to spook her. She might take the first train out of town if he did that. But he also couldn't deny his growing feelings, and hoped they got this train robber business done and over with sooner than later. Otherwise, he was liable to kiss her again.

21

Goldie spent the rest of the day helping Bella in the house. She learned more about the farm, Bella and Calvin's adventurous first year (which also involved some dangerous situations) and the answer to a burning question: what was it like for her and the other women on the farm who came here as mail-order brides?

"It was exciting and frightening all at the same time," Bella explained. "But everything worked out for everyone involved."

Goldie thought of Theodore and wondered if she'd have found the same happiness with him had he not been shot by the train robbers. Would they have had a good life in Seattle? Work was waiting for them, and she felt bad not asking which sawmill father and son would have been working. She could have written mill owners, told them what happened, then asked for a job. Maybe they needed a bookkeeper. She was good with numbers, always had been...

"You are lucky to be here," Bella said, breaking into her thoughts.

Goldie nodded. "Lucky to be alive, you mean."

"Yes, of course, but to be here in this place with so many wonderful people. Why do you not stay?"

Her mind raced. Had she told Bella about her plans to leave? The last twenty-four hours had been a blur, and she still had the sense of not knowing if she was coming or going. "I… I'll have to go. If I can figure out where Ben Ferguson was to be employed, I might find work there."

Bella heaved a sigh. "I wish you would try to find work in Nowhere first."

"What work? I don't sew well enough to ask for work at the dressmaker's. The town doesn't employ a librarian, not that it would make a difference, considering the size of your library. And as far as I know, no one else is hiring."

"Have you asked?"

"I didn't have to. Connie told me."

"Ah, yes, dear Connie." Bella smiled. "She's not one to keep you on either. You know that, don't you? As soon as you cost her money, she'll have no more need of you. Everything depends on how good her business is going, and few people stay at the hotel." She smiled. "Other than us when a good amount of us go to Nowhere. But people passing through, they'd rather sleep on the train and go on to Seattle or Portland."

Goldie sighed. "She told me the same." She forced a smile. "I guess I'm leaving once I have the funds."

Bella smiled sympathetically. "I wish you the best of luck. And if Connie decides she can no longer afford to pay you, you could always come here and find work."

Goldie's eyebrows shot up. "On the farm?"

"Sure. You could finish out the harvest or help Ebba with the children. She's not only Daniel's wife, but the farm school-teacher. We even plan to build a schoolhouse. Right now, the chapel doubles as the school."

Goldie couldn't believe it—she was offering her a job?

"That's amazing. A farm with its own chapel, school, and train station."

Bella grinned. "And preacher."

She smiled back. "Do you have weddings here?"

"Oh, yes. We've had quite a few." She poured Goldie a cup of coffee and gave it to her.

"Thank you." Goldie took a sip, reveling in the hot brew despite the warm morning.

"And who knows," Bella said on her way back to the stove. "You could find a gentleman, fall in love and marry."

Despite the warmth, a chill went up Goldie's spine. "I don't know about that."

Bella turned to her. "Don't you want to get married?"

"I did, but I wanted to marry for love. Desperation made me become a mail-order bride."

"And so it did to many of us." Bella sat at the table with her. "Myself included." She leaned toward her. "You could find love here."

Goldie shuddered. She wanted to believe, but nothing was certain. For crying out loud, she just wanted to leave Bella's house without getting shot at. How could she think of all the things they just talked about on top of that? She didn't have the energy to and wanted to change the subject. Losing her parents, losing Theodore and his father, and losing the dream that had kept her going all this time… to resurrect it could only mean more pain, and she didn't think she could take anymore.

She finished her coffee, feeling overwhelmed. She didn't know what to say, but she knew Bella was right. This place had everything she could ever want: a sense of community, a purpose, and a chance to start over. But she couldn't help the nagging feeling that she needed to keep moving forward.

She should go through the Fergusons' things again. Maybe she missed something. A small piece of paper with a name, an address, anything that would tell her where Mr. Ferguson and his son were to report for work.

"Think about staying," Bella said. "That's all I ask."

Goldie smiled and nodded but said nothing. The thought of staying frightened her. There was so little here, and her prospects would be limited to a few single cowhands as far as marriage went. And what would the work be like? Would she be working her fingers to the bone day in and day out?

Bella must have sensed her hesitation. She stood and patted her on the back. "Don't worry. I know you have a lot on your mind, but just remember that you always have a home here if you need it."

Goldie smiled, grateful for the kindness she'd received since arriving. She knew she would always remember this place and the people who helped her when she needed it most. She just hoped she didn't need it again too soon. Maybe by now the train robbers had moved on and so could she.

"Why don't you go upstairs and rest before lunch?" Bella suggested.

"Thank you, I think I will." Goldie left the table and headed for the stairs. As she went to her room, she mulled over Bella's offer. Maybe she should consider staying longer. She could help at the hotel, then on the farm until she had enough money to move on. And who knows, maybe she could fall in love and start a new life here.

Rhys popped into her head. After all, there was nothing wrong with giving it a chance, was there? Her primary concern had been to keep everyone safe. But if the Coolidges had left the area, she was free to concentrate on creating a new life for herself.

The thought made Goldie smile, and for the first time since she'd lost everything, she felt a glimmer of hope. She would think about it some more, but for now she needed to keep her head down and focus on finding out where Ben and Theodore were supposed to be working. At least then she'd still have the opportunity to start over in Seattle if she needed. Even if she couldn't work for the company that hired the Fergusons, they might know of somewhere she could.

The only problem was, Rhys kept popping into her head every time she thought of leaving.

RHYS TRIED to concentrate on picking apples, but his heart wasn't in it. He should be back at Calvin and Bella's guarding Goldie.

"Wipe that look off yer face," Calvin said. "This isn't so bad."

Rhys reached for another apple, put it in the bag slung over his shoulder, then started his descent down the ladder. "I'm surprised you can see my face." When he reached the ground, he carefully emptied the bag into the empty bushel basket, then glanced toward the farm.

"We want to give the impression that everything's fine," Calvin said. "None of us are gonna cower in the barn today. Yesterday they might have thought we were scared and come back."

"Then we'll catch them." Rhys prepared to climb up the ladder again.

Calvin took his arm. "Yer bein' awful protective of the lady. Sure there ain't more goin' on than ya think?"

Rhys looked at the hand on his arm. "What do you mean?"

Calvin smiled and winked at his sons Thatcher and Alastair helped pick while some of their cousins were patrolling the area. "Only that it's becomin' apparent yer sweet on her. So when are ya gonna do somethin' 'bout it?"

Rhys gaped at him a moment. Was it that obvious? "I, er, I have no idea." He sighed. "Besides, she's determined to leave as soon as she can."

"Because she don't see no other way to survive," Calvin

said. "If'n it's in yer heart to have her stay, then say somethin'. She'll be able to see the man ya are if'n she ain't got all that fear hangin' over her. She's runnin', Rhys, 'cause she's scared."

His eyes widened. "Have you seen that woman shoot? She's a better shot than I am. In fact, I'd wager she's a better shot than you."

Alastair and Thatcher laughed and went up another tree.

Rhys watched them, then turned back to Calvin. "I know she's scared," he said, his voice softening. "And I want to help her. But I don't know if I can give her what she needs." He looked at his feet. "Sometimes I don't even know if I can protect her. What if those train robbers come back? What if they hurt her?"

"Ya cain't focus on the what-ifs," Calvin said firmly. "All ya can do is try. And I think ya owe it to yerself to do just that." He clapped Rhys on the shoulder. "Now, why don't ya take a break? Yer no good to anyone if yer all mopey."

Rhys nodded and headed to the main farmhouse. When he reached it, some of Thatcher and Alastair's cousins were gathered around a couple of long tables cleaning their guns. He smiled at their ingenuity. They were putting on a show if indeed the train robbers were nearby. The Coolidges were outmanned and outgunned, and this was the Weavers way of letting them know.

"Hello," Sebastian called. "How's it going in the orchard?"

"Fine, as far as I know. Ulysses and Daniel Jr. and some cowhands are scouting the perimeter of the orchards and pastures closest to the houses and barns."

"Ah, good." Sebastian smiled. "You know, I've been meaning to talk to you."

Rhys raised an eyebrow. "About what?"

Sebastian leaned in as the other men smiled. "Miss Colson."

Rhys groaned. "Is it that obvious?"

The other men chuckled.

"Only to everyone in a five-mile radius. Look, Rhys, I know you're worried about her. But you can't just sit around and wait for something to happen. You need to take action."

"I know," Rhys said. "But she's lost everything and everyone she's ever cared about. I don't want to add to that by making her feel like she has to stay here for me. For all I know, she has no interest in me." He thought of the sweetness of their kiss and snapped his mouth shut. None of them needed to know about that.

"Yer a fool if ya think she ain't already stayin' for ya," Calvin said with a grin. Rhys hadn't heard him come up behind him. "I see the way she looks at ya when she thinks no one is watchin'. And the way ya look at her when *you* think no one is."

Rhys felt a warmth spread through his chest at the thought of Goldie staying for his sake. But he couldn't let himself get too carried away. "Like I said, I don't want to force her into anything she doesn't want."

"Ya don't have to force her," Sebastian said. "Just be there for her. Listen to her when she talks, be a shoulder for her to lean on. Those are the things that matter. After all, sometimes a person needs more than just safety. They need to feel wanted and loved."

Rhys thought about it for a moment. Maybe Calvin and Sebastian were right. He didn't have to do anything grand or sweeping to win Goldie over. Maybe he just had to be there for her, to show her the sort of man he was. "Thanks, Sebastian. I'll keep that in mind."

Sebastian clapped him on the back. "Good man."

Rhys watched as Sebastian went back to cleaning his rifle. He knew deep down that Sebastian was right. Goldie needed more than just a haven. She needed someone to rely on, someone to share her life with. And he wanted to be that person. He just didn't know how to tell her.

He sighed and leaned against a tree, looking out at the

farm. Maybe he could show her, rather than tell her. Maybe he could protect her and make her feel safe while also showing that he cared for her. It was worth a shot at least. He straightened up and headed back to the main farmhouse to speak to Harlan. Then he'd find Goldie and show her he was there for her.

He stopped up short as he realized there was only one way to do it. "Oh, boy," he breathed. He closed his eyes a moment, sent up a silent prayer, then headed for the house.

22

Goldie got up after an hour, ate lunch with Bella and her daughter-in-laws Mia and Selena, then slipped her pistol into her apron pocket and headed for the sorting barn. She hadn't seen Phoebe since breakfast. Bella said she was spending the day at the main farmhouse to help Granny Mary with some things.

She was still tired as she and the women went to the barn, and noticed they weren't without escort. Some men were always nearby, and she still couldn't get over how they were doing all this for her. The thought made her want to stay in Nowhere. The people on this farm and in town were kind and looked out for one another. Would she find that in cities the size of Seattle, Portland, or San Francisco?

She shook her head as she walked. No, she wouldn't, but staying here still didn't solve the problem of making a life for herself. There was no work in town other than the hotel, and who knew how long that would last? Out here, there might be work, but when it came to finding a husband one day, there was no guarantee she would. The same went for Nowhere.

And there was still the problem of the Coolidge brothers. They might leave her alone for now, but that didn't mean they wouldn't come back and try again. It was a distinct possibility, and one she'd have to face sooner or later. Had anyone else thought of that? She was sure they had and were keeping it to themselves for her benefit, afraid they'd scare her. Too late. She was scared enough as it was.

So, she was right back to square one. The best course of action she could take if she wanted to keep those around her safe, not to mention herself, was to get as far away from Nowhere and the Weaver farm as she could. Maybe one day, if she was lucky, she'd find someone to fall in love with, and a place she felt at peace. She was having that here with the Weavers and people of Nowhere when someone took a shot at her.

When they reached the sorting barn, she heard a shout. "Goldie!" Rhys called from the house. He started for them.

Bella smiled. "He's such a handsome man, don't you think?"

Tears stung Goldie's eyes. "Handsome can't save you from a bullet."

Bella scoffed. "You are so stubborn. Look at his eyes. They are for you." She entered the barn with the others.

Goldie sighed. She didn't want to upset Bella, but she didn't see what she could do. Just because the man stole a kiss from her last night didn't mean he wanted anything more, and she didn't have time to stay and find out if he did. It was too risky. The last thing she wanted was to be walking down Nowhere's main street and get shot at by the likes of Herbert Coolidge, only to have him hit Rhys instead of her.

He reached her and smiled. "Goldie, do you have a minute?"

She glanced at the barn and back. "They've started sorting."

"I know, but I need to talk to you." He took her arm and went to the nearest tree. She noted they were between the barn and the tree, with plenty of people around. If someone tried to shoot her, they'd have a hard time of it. She hoped.

He looked into her eyes. "I… well, I wanted to tell you…"

There was a shout, then another, followed by her worst nightmare: gunfire.

"Get down!" Rhys shoved her to the ground and shielded her with his body.

"No," she yelled, fearing the worst. What if they hit Rhys?

Men came running from the barn as some women quickly herded children into it. Rhys, bent over her, took a quick look around. "Hurry, let's get you into the barn." He pulled her to her feet, took her arm with one hand and pulled his gun with the other. "Now!"

They ran as more shots rang out. They were coming from one of the orchards. Goldie was vaguely aware of a saddled horse running through the barnyard without a rider. Had one of the Weavers or townsfolk hit one of the train robbers?

They reached the barn and ran inside. As soon as they were in, Rhys and Clinton Cooke pulled the doors closed, then hurried to shut the doors at the other end of the structure. Doing so plunged the barn into darkness.

Goldie blinked a few times as her eyes adjusted to the dim light. Some of the children whimpered. Then everything fell silent. "What's happening?"

"Quiet," Bella hissed. "Our men will take care of it. Children, get into the stalls, stay away from the doors."

There was a scamper of feet as they did what she asked.

"Rhys, take Goldie into the hayloft. They can't shoot at her up there unless they're in a tree." Bella headed for the doors at the far end.

"Where are you going?" Goldie asked.

Bella smiled. "To get some guns." She ducked into a stall and emerged with two rifles.

"Give me one of those," Goldie said.

Bella glanced at Rhys, who nodded. "She's a crack shot. Do it."

She handed Goldie a rifle then took up a position off to one side of a window that overlooked the barnyard and the main farmhouse.

Rhys steered Goldie to the hayloft's ladder and took the rifle from her. "Up you go."

She scrambled up, then reached down and took the rifle as he handed it up. As soon as he joined her, he motioned her to stay, then crept to the open loft doors on his hands and knees.

Goldie followed, lowering herself to her belly the closer she got.

"What are you doing?" he whispered.

"I was going to ask you the same thing."

He glanced at the rifle in her hand. "I wanted to see why it was so quiet."

She listened, heard nothing, then passed him, creeping closer to the end of the loft.

"Goldie," he hissed. "Get back here."

She looked over her shoulder at him. "If we stay low, they won't see us from down there. Besides, if I see one of them, I'm going to stop them."

He crawled to where she'd planted herself. She could look out over the orchard before them and see part of the barnyard and the chapel. Two long tables had been set up on the yard, but she didn't know what for. From this distance, all she could see were a few small cans of something and some cloths.

"Goldie," Rhys whispered.

"Yes?" she whispered back.

"This might not be the best time, but what I wanted to say earlier was… I'm here for you."

She looked at him as her heart warmed. "Yes. I know."

He shook his head. "That didn't come out right. You know I'm here for you, but I want to be there for you in other ways."

She scanned the orchards and saw nothing. It was as if

everyone outside had disappeared in a puff of smoke. She made a face as the pink pistol poked her in the hip every time she moved. "Uh-huh."

He reached over, tucked his finger under her chin and turned her face toward his. "Goldie…"

She looked into his eyes and saw something only hinted at the night before. "Rhys?"

"You were a mail-order bride when you came to town."

She nodded. "That's right."

He scooted closer. "And you became one because you saw no other way to survive."

Heat crept into her cheeks. "Yes."

Rhys wiggled closer. "Did you love him?"

"I only knew him a couple of days."

"But you were ready to marry him."

"Yes." She glanced at the orchards. It was awfully quiet out there, which made her nervous. What if one of them was circling back this way to cause trouble?

"Sweetheart."

She looked at him, her heart in her throat. "What?"

He put a hand on her head as he drew closer. The kiss was warm, gentle, and sent her senses reeling. A tiny sound escaped, and she realized it came from her. Soon one of his arms came around her, pulling her flush against him as he deepened the kiss.

Goldie didn't know what to think. Wasn't he concerned about the train robbers? Shouldn't she be at this point? But they were out of sight, and the only ones that knew they were up here were the people in the barn below. This was probably the safest place they could be.

When she realized that, she enjoyed the kiss, and soon found herself kissing him back!

When Rhys finally drew back, he smiled then held her close. "Goldie," he whispered. "I know we haven't known each other long, but if you can come all this way to put your life into the hands of a complete stranger, can you find it in your heart to do the same for me?"

They were nose to nose as she gazed into his eyes. "Rhys, what are you saying?"

He smiled. "That I'm falling in love with you and want to keep you safe the best way I know how. Will you marry me?"

For a moment she thought her heart would jump right out of her chest. "You... want to marry me?" She realized she hadn't whispered and snapped her mouth shut.

"With all my heart." He'd stopped whispering too. "No one should have to face this world alone, and I'd be a fool to keep living mine without someone like you. I don't want you to leave Nowhere. Stay, become my wife, and share with me what my life has to..." he rolled back to put some distance between them. "What is that?"

She looked down, smiled, and pulled the pistol from her pocket. She set it aside. "You were saying?"

He smiled and pulled her against him. "I was saying, share with me all that my life has to offer."

Tears filled her eyes. He was falling in love with her? She stared at him wide eyed. Her biggest fear in becoming a mail-order bride was marrying someone who wouldn't love her back. She had a lot of love to give, and to not have it recipro-cated might well kill her. She also feared the opposite happen-ing. But if Rhys was saying he loved her... she swallowed hard, sniffed back tears, and looked him in the eyes. Great Scott! Did she love Rhys?

Goldie laughed.

"What's so funny?"

She shook her head. "Oh, dear me. But I'm falling in love with you too!"

Bella said something in Italian below them, and several people snorted with laughter.

Goldie gasped. "They can hear us."

He nodded. "Mm-hmm." He slid his other arm under her

neck and held her close. "And they'll hear this too. Goldie Colson, you'd make me the happiest man in the world if you'd become my wife. We're already on our way to being what the other needs, and I promise no silly train robber is going to come between us. Besides, if I can't protect us, you can."

She laughed. So did everyone else in the barn. "Yes, Rhys," she whispered. "I'll marry you."

A cheer went up from down below as a shot fired outside the barn.

Goldie jumped in Rhys' arms, then noticed he was smiling. "What is it?"

He unwrapped his arms from around her, then looked outside. "Calvin."

"What?" She looked too and laughed.

The Coolidge brothers and their cousin Dilbert were lined up in front of the barn, their hands tied behind their backs. "Don't tell me we're the cause of all that sappy talk from the hayloft," one of them said. Was it Herbert? Goldie peered at him. Could be—he was taller than the one next to him, who had the same eyes. That had to be Dale. The third had a craggy face. She recognized it from the wanted poster Spencer showed her when she first got to town.

The train robbers looked at one another and scowled as Rhys pulled her to her feet. "You think that was sappy? I'll show you sappy." He pulled Goldie into his arms and kissed her soundly.

"Well, about time," Hoskins said from somewhere below.

"You said it." That was Arlan, Goldie was sure of it. Of course, by this time she didn't care who said what. There was only Rhys, his kiss, and the knowledge that what she'd been longing for was right in front of her, but her fear kept her from seeing it. Rhys had opened her eyes, and she was so glad she'd looked.

When he broke the kiss, Herbert, Dale and Dilbert acted as

though they were going to be sick as Arlan and some of the other men hauled them off to who knows where.

Goldie held onto Rhys, let her tears fall, and spied the pink pistol in the hay. She smiled. One tragedy brought her to this place while another brought her a man who would truly love her. "I do love you," she said against him. "I didn't want to, but I do."

He smiled at her. "I know, and I love you. Now what do you say to letting Leona Riley and Betsy Quinn outfit you for a wedding?"

She smiled back as her happy tears fell. "I say, let them have the best time they've ever had preparing a bride."

The Weaver farm chapel, one week later...

Harvest time on the Weaver farm took every pair of hands, so Goldie thought it only right that she and Rhys marry on the farm so the Weavers could attend without losing valuable work time. The little church was filled to the brim with Weavers and folks from town, and Goldie couldn't get over the outpouring of kindness from everyone.

She also couldn't get over how one passenger from the train had dropped one of her belongings, and Ben Ferguson had picked it up but wasn't sure to whom it belonged. Mrs. Clara Dinwiddie ran into Connie and Hoskins at Hank's restaurant, and they got to talking. They'd heard about the pink pistol from Goldie, who did a little target practice with it when she gave Rhys some pointers one afternoon amidst making wedding plans.

Now Mrs. Dinwiddie sat in the back row of the chapel, and Goldie wondered if she had the pink pistol with her. The woman wanted her to write a little something on the parchment that came with it. She still didn't see how a pistol brought Rhys into her life and thank goodness she didn't have to use it during those few days at the farm when the Coolidges tried to exact their revenge. Instead, Rhys Miller had set out to protect her and was doing so the best he knew how. As her husband.

"And do you, Rhys Jonathan Miller, take Goldie Rebecca Colson to be your lawfully wedded wife?"

Rhys looked into her eyes. "I do."

"Then by the power vested in me by the state of Washington, I now pronounce you man and wife." Pastor Wingate smiled. "You may kiss the bride."

Rhys smiled at her, pulled her into his arms and kissed her with everything he had.

Goldie melted against him. If they were falling in love a week ago, they had arrived by today. She never thought she'd find the deep love she knew she could give and was now married to a man equally capable of returning it.

Folks cheered as they broke the kiss and made their way down the aisle. Goldie caught sight of Mrs. Dinwiddie and smiled at her. The woman was already leaving the pew, intent on following them. "Rhys," Goldie said over the cacophony of congratulations and well wishes. "I need to speak with Mrs. Dinwiddie."

"What? Now?"

She nodded. "I know she's taking the afternoon train—it will be here soon."

"Very well. Shall I go with you?"

"No, she's coming over here."

Goldie smiled as the older woman slipped through the surrounding crowd, her valise in her hands. "Congratulations, my dear. Can I see you for a moment? I must head to the train platform."

"Of course." Goldie steered her through the well-wishers

and back into the chapel. Several more people hugged her on the way out, and soon things were calm enough for her to say goodbye to Clara Dinwiddie. "Goodness, what a day. Thank you for coming, and I'm sorry about your pistol."

"Oh, that's all right, dear. I set it on a bench at the train station in Baker City, and don't know what I was thinking walking off like that. But it all turned out in the end. I'm so glad your Mr. Ferguson picked it up. He must have seen me wander off without it." She pulled the beautiful mahogany box out of her valise and set it on a pew. "Now, if you don't mind, could you write a little something?"

Goldie smiled. "Oh, um, but ma'am, I don't think…"

"Please, dear." She opened the box, pulled the piece of parchment from a sleeve in the green velvet lining and handed it to her. She took a pen from her reticule and gave her that too.

Goldie stared at them. "You're serious."

"Of course, dear."

Goldie gave her a perplexed look, shrugged, then using the pistol's box as a writing surface, scribbled something on the parchment.

"Don't forget to add your wedding date," Mrs. Dinwiddie reminded her.

Goldie smiled. "Of course not." She finished writing and handed the parchment back.

The old woman took it, smiled, put the parchment back in the case and closed it. "Now if you don't mind, I have a train to catch." She started to leave.

"Mrs. Dinwiddie," Goldie said, just as perplexed as before. "Where are you going?"

She smiled as she put the case into her valise. "Oh, I have relatives and friends all over. Washington, South Dakota, Texas. I try to visit everyone." She smiled again. "Goodbye, my dear." Without another word, she left the chapel.

Rhys came back in. "Where is she going?"

Goldie stared after her. "To catch her train."

He kissed her on the cheek. "Lucky for Mrs. Dinwiddie, she happened to run into Connie and Hoskins that day at Hank's. Otherwise, she'd have never gotten her pistol back."

Goldie nodded. "She thinks it brings people together."

He shrugged. "We're together."

"Yes, but you hardly saw the thing. I had it with me that day the Coolidge brothers attacked the train, but couldn't even use it."

"Thank goodness it still did its job." He pulled her close, looked into her eyes, and smiled. "I love you, Mrs. Miller."

She returned his smile. "I love you too."

"Are you ready for our wedding feast?"

"Kiss me first."

Rhys lowered his face to hers and did. It was the most wondrous kiss yet.

But in the back of her mind, Goldie Miller saw that pink-handled pistol and a smiling Mrs. Dinwiddie.

BULLSEYE BRIDE

By Kari Trumbo

1

A shiver ran up Kitty's spine as she touched the cloudy glass of the pawnshop's front window. Beyond it, barely visible, was a dark wooden case with the items that would be available for sale in one week if the owner didn't pay back his loan. Even though she had only one dollar to her name, she wanted what was in that wooden case more than almost anything.

She shook the desire from her shoulders and straightened her spine. How childish. She should want her father's return more than the beautiful pearl-handled pistol nestled within the green velvet–lined wooden box. He'd been gone for over two months, and Ma speculated he was dead—not that his loss seemed to change her day much.

Other than the fact that they couldn't pay to live in their house.

Kitty's threadbare coat, borrowed from Ma, did little to keep out the chill of the wind blowing over the Black Hills and down into Deadwood Gulch. Spring was on the way, but not quite there yet. Summer would mean she could hunt more easily and they wouldn't need so much wood for the stove. Her four brothers were a big help, but without Pa there to provide, their storage of store-bought staples was gone. No money left for a pink pistol, no matter how pretty it might be.

No, her pocket held just enough to enter the Deadwood Annual Shooting Contest. Thad Easton's printed poster hung inside the window, just out of the way enough to still see the goods on the shelves. That fact mattered little because she knew what the sheet said by heart. The competition was in fourteen days, and she hadn't signed up yet. Mainly because she'd had to find the time to do odd jobs around town until she'd earned the highly expensive entry fee of a whole dollar.

Kitty clenched her fist and reached for the door just as a large masculine hand did the same. It brushed across hers, making her shiver slightly and jump. Where had he come from? Looking up, her vision caught and held on the man she'd just been thinking about. Thad Easton smiled at her and held the door open.

"Katherine, good to see you in town."

She swallowed hard. How was she to reply to that? She only came into town to go to church and to sell the pelts of the rabbits and other small animals she caught for food around their house, though the few pennies those sales brought in were barely enough to buy flour. "Good to see you, too." She swallowed hard again. The man was far too handsome, and wealthy, for her to go all doe-eyed, but her heart raced all the same.

Her words made Thad's smile grow even more. "Are you here to sign up for the contest? None of the other ladies will bother if you don't. There is no competition without you."

He'd noticed? Warmth spread over her cheeks as she ducked in the door and out of the street.

"Now, Thad, don't you let your words go to Kitty's head. That sheriff's wife from over in Belle Fourche has already signed up, and I hear she's a crack shot," Dalton said.

Kitty rushed to the front of the shop to look at the signup sheet. Sure enough, her friend Hannah Longfellow had signed up to compete. Hannah had teased her husband, Blake, for years about driving a car wherever he needed to go instead of riding a horse, but that very thing allowed Hannah to have friends in other towns.

"I couldn't compete against Hannah." Kitty bit her lip. Well, she could, but she wouldn't want to. Especially since there was no prize for the women's competition. Hannah was her closest friend, and the shot was a measly thirty yards. Barely a challenge.

"You mean you're not going to enter?" Dalton, the pawn-broker, leaned over the counter and smacked his lips, shoving his wad of tobacco deeper into his cheek with his tongue. "You out of money, ain't ya?" Greed narrowed his eyes. "I'm sure we could find something in that hovel worth the dollar entry fee."

Thad held up his hand. "Dalton, don't put words in her mouth or start taking an inventory of her goods before she needs your unique...services." His lip curled, making Kitty wonder why he'd put the signup only in the pawn shop if he didn't want to come in here.

"Maybe you have some money?" Dalton poked her arm hard enough to shove her back into Thad, who righted her immediately, but not before the flutters in her stomach had taken flight. Dalton growled like she'd moved intentionally and pushed the sheet toward her. "I don't think Mrs. Longfellow would mind a little friendly competition."

Kitty took a step back away from the counter and Dalton's poking finger. "Honestly, I only came in to look more closely at the pistol in the window. Mine has seen better days." Not that she could replace it. Ma had warned her if she didn't win the elite shooting competition, they would have to go live with Pa's brother, Damion Horwath—their only living relative. Ma was purposely hiding their situation from Damion for as long as possible, but he would find out about Pa soon enough.

"That pistol ain't for sale just yet. The owner was in need of ticket money to get to Texas. He promised he'd be back in time to claim it. His date isn't up for two whole days yet." Dalton snickered. "If you have money, might as well put it to good use. That dollar will help fund the—" He stopped talking as she held up her hand.

"I can read the sign," Kitty said. Though Dalton probably assumed she couldn't. She stored away the information on the exact date the pistol would be available for later. The cost was beyond what she could afford anyway, especially with the entry fee that had to be paid or she would lose everything. "Why are there never any women in the elite competition?" she asked. If they wanted her to join the women's so badly, why couldn't she shoot against the men instead and win the prize money needed to save her family?

"A woman?" Dalton laughed and slapped the counter so loudly Kitty jumped. "You think a woman could beat out Thad or Amos? Not likely. Those two bring all the money. Every year we wait to see who's a better shot."

Thad flattened his lips. "Or to see which shooter the wind favors that year. I think Amos and I are equally matched. Maybe adding in a new contender would bring about a little excitement. It couldn't hurt. The project from the proceeds is huge this year. We need all the entries we can get."

Dalton snorted and tugged the sheet out of reach. "But not by contending against a woman. There's no way to win that. Either the man will claim he let her win to honor her or to save face, *or* they would just drop out of the running and refuse to compete. I can promise you, put a woman's name on that elite shooter list and no one will come because they'll assume there won't be a contest at all." He slammed his finger down on the entry sheet for good measure.

Kitty tried to school her features and prayed neither man could read on her face how she felt. Dalton could just as well have punched her. Without that money, her home and her freedom were gone. She raced for the door before either man could see her tears. In a blur, she took in the shiny wooden box and beautiful pearl-handled pistol once more. It would never be hers.

#

Thad watched Katherine race from the pawnshop, dash past the window, and disappear out of sight.

"It ain't right, Thad. That girl shouldn't have to hunt to provide food for that family," Dalton said, his tone changing to one of worry.

Thad swallowed the acrid words that wanted to burst forth. Dalton had been downright cruel to the girl he apparently felt sorry for. "She can't help that her father is a treacherous heathen who cheated the snake trappers near the Badlands."

Dalton winced, showing large gaps of missing teeth. "I hadn't heard what happened to him. How do you know?"

"I don't. I just heard him bragging as he was waiting for his missus outside of church right before he disappeared. He said he was going to the Badlands to skunk a few skunks. Since he hasn't returned yet, I would assume they had the same idea and caught up with him first."

"That leaves Mrs. Horwath in a bad place. Five kids, not that Kitty's a child anymore."

No, she certainly wasn't. Kitty's pink cheeks and lovely blonde hair made her very appealing to look at, but her quick wit, precise aim with a pistol, and her father's standing in the community made her an unacceptable mate for most men who were either looking for no more attachment than a sporting gal or had money and were looking for a gentle woman to escape the rough edges of Deadwood in their homes.

While Thad was of the latter set himself, he hadn't found any of the few wealthy ladies in town to suit him. Their fathers had invited him out for cigars and wanted to know all about his lumber investments, but knowing what they were about, he offered little information. The dealings with these fathers felt no deeper than picking a cow for butchering. If they didn't know what his affairs were like, then they couldn't pester him as much.

"That pistol she was talking about… It truly is unique. I'm not surprised it caught her eye," Thad said. He strode toward the case, and Dalton followed on his heels like a starving dog. Dalton licked his lips, accentuating the vision.

"It is. I think those are genuine pearl handles. Very rare to see anything like them. And that case, very well made. I'm sure I'll get more for it than I lent."

Thad eyed the unscrupulous man. "After two more days."

"Of course." Dalton squirmed slightly, then backed away a few paces. "I'm an honest man, Thad. You know that."

Thad kept his feelings to himself, as he tried to often do. "Who else is signed up for the contest? It's only two weeks away, and the need for the roller rink is great. There's only so much I can donate as far as the cost of lumber. I have to pay my men."

Dalton whistled through his teeth. "Not great enough to have women shooting more than they already are. I know Kitty was the one who argued with Slade to get a women's division in the first place, but that's not why people come."

"You don't think so? Slade didn't want to then, but he's glad he made the exception now."

"Don't you dare let her sign up and put all my hard work of rounding people up go to waste. If you want everyone but the women to drop out, you let her sign up. And while you're at it, you'd best go borrow the dunce cap from the school because people will be laughing at you up one side of the street and down the other. They'll remember you for genera-tions as the one who slowed down progress in Deadwood. And let's face it, progress is pretty slow as it is."

Thad couldn't deny it. So many people wanted Deadwood to stay rough and tumble. Judging by Dalton's immediate reaction, he felt so, too. Life wasn't fair, and this situation was particularly unfair. Unlike any of the other contestants, himself most of all, Katherine needed the money so that her family could buy foodstuffs and necessities. Her coat had looked more thread than fabric. Winning might not save them, but it would go a long way toward helping the whole family get back on their feet.

"I'm not making any decision like that without Mr. Slade. So don't get your dander up." Thad adjusted his hat, ready to head back to work.

Dalton nodded and tapped the tip of his pencil on the paper. "She still didn't sign up for the women's contest. You don't think she's so bad off that she won't?"

Thad didn't answer right away. Despite what Dalton professed, watching Katherine shoot was pure joy. She had a talent and charm that made watching her pure fun. You couldn't help but cheer for her. She reminded him a little of the stories of Annie Oakley from years before. Though even Katherine would say she wasn't as crack of a shot as Annie.

"I can't say. I hope she does."

Scanning the list from a distance, Thad recognized all the names on the men's list and the two names on the women's list. He and Amos were the only men signed up for the elite contest. There were cash prizes for the men's and elite, but nothing for the women's. Women weren't supposed to compete, though Thad thought the lack of a prize for the women was purely greed on Mr. Slade's part.

"I wouldn't bother the banker with asking him about Kitty," Dalton said. "She annoys him and he'll say no. Especially with how her father isn't here. He probably hasn't made his bank payment in two months since he disappeared. So, Slade is not going to extend a hand to Kitty or any of her family."

If only there were another way, Thad wondered. But he'd been given the task of enriching the town and making it a better place for families to live with the proceeds that came from the annual shooting contest. Last year, he'd been able to purchase new much-needed desks for the school. The year before that, he'd been able to buy new hymnals for the two new churches in town.

Enrichment. Not charity. As much as he'd like to help the Horwaths and especially Katherine, his hands were firmly tied. "You're probably right," he said. "But you're also right in that we have to do something to help the Horwaths. They are part of this community and have lived right outside of town for longer than I can remember."

"Her pa came in 1889 when his wife was round with Kitty in her belly." Dalton laughed, wheezed, then spit a wad of chew across the room, hitting a brass spittoon behind the counter. "Kitty looks a lot like her mom did then. Like a willow tree with light hair." He laughed again.

The vision of Katherine in a light-green dress like the delicate willow branches near the river filled Thad's thoughts, and he headed for the door almost as fast as Katherine had. He couldn't help her, not when it came to the competition. No matter how much he wanted to.

Books in the Pink Pistol Sisterhood Series

In Her Sights by **Karen Witemeyer**
Book 1 ~ March 30
Love on Target **by Shanna Hatfield**
Book 2 ~ April 10
Love Under Fire **by Cheryl Pierson**
Book 3 ~ April 20
Bulletproof Bride **by Kit Morgan**
Book 4 ~ April 30
Bullseye Bride **by Kari Trumbo**
Book 5 ~ May 10
Disarming His Heart **by Winnie Griggs**
Book 6 ~ May 20
One Shot at Love **by Linda Broday**
Book 7 ~ May 30
Armed & Marvelous **by Pam Crooks**
Book 8 ~ June 10
Lucky Shot **by Jeannie Watt**
Book 9 ~ June 20
Aiming for His Heart **by Julie Benson**
Book 10 ~ June 30
Pistol Perfect **by Jessie Gussman**
Book 11 ~ July 10

See all the Pink Pistol Sisterhood Books at
www.petticoatsandpistols.com.

ABOUT THE AUTHOR

Kit Morgan has written for fun all of her life. Whether she's writing contemporary or historical romance, her whimsical stories are fun, inspirational, sweet and clean, and depict a strong sense of family and community. Raised by a homicide detective, one would think she'd write suspense, (and yes, she plans to get around to those eventually, cozy mysteries too!) but Kit likes fun and romantic westerns! Kit lives in the beautiful Pacific Northwest in a little log cabin on Clear Creek, after which her fictional town that appears in many of her books is named.

WANT TO GET IN ON THE FUN?

Find out about new releases, cover reveals, bonus content, fun times and more! Sign up for Kit's newsletter at www.authorkitmorgan.com

Printed in Great Britain
by Amazon